A. E. Van Vogt

The Mind Cage

Panther

Granada Publishing Limited
First published in Great Britain in 1960 by
Panther Books Ltd
Frogmore, St Albans, Herts AL2 2NF
Reprinted 1963, 1968, 1975

Copyright © A. E. Van Vogt 1957
Made and printed in Great Britain by
Cox & Wyman Ltd, London, Reading and Fakenham
Set in Intertype Plantin

The Mind Cage

CHAPTER ONE

David Marin bit his lip as the chairman of the Group Masters said, 'and now, the case of Wade Trask, guilty of sedition.'

Marin had been listening unwillingly to Group Master John Peeler, who – after a year – was still trying to convince council members that a change should be made in the group law about women. It was a well-known 'secret' that Peeler had become particularly attached to a young woman and that he was striving to have a special category set up which would keep the girl out of the group mating games.

Marin turned away from the whispered argument, because – *Wade Trask, guilty of sedition.* It was the case he had been waiting for. Marin let his gaze drift around the council room. There were a dozen other men and two recording secretaries sitting at the long table. Oscar Podrage, the heavy-set, grim young man who was Group Master of Middle North America, looked up and said, 'Is this that scientist?'

Medellin, the chairman, nodded at one of the two secretaries. The clerk glanced through some papers and then read out: 'Wade Trask, Physical Engineer, Authority on Pripps, Electronics Experimentalist—' He broke off. 'There's a list of books he's written.'

Chairman Medellin was glancing from face to face. 'We seem to be in agreement, gentlemen,' he said. And there was just a hint of relief in his voice.

Marin raised his hand, and had the floor. Thoughtfully, he studied his audience. Of those present, Podrage, Edmund Slater, Medellin and himself were career men. The others had been industrial, educational and scientific leaders before being invited to take the exalted positions which they now held. Medellin and Podrage were the supreme organizers of this age which combined group living with free enterprise. Slater, the policeman, was their sword and whip. And David Marin was – what?

He didn't quite belong among these earthy men.

As the commander of all the armed forces of the immortal

Great Judge, he provided the human stuff which the others molded and tailored, in their remorseless fashion.

His job: to conquer one by one, or in groups, those 'bandit' states that had sprung up all over the world after the third atomic war, which had ended more than a score of years before. Having done so, he turned the conquered people over to the organizers and to the policeman-executioner. And stepped back, aloof, no longer concerned.

It had always made him a man apart in this council. Perhaps that would stand against him now, for he knew there was jealousy, and rancor, and fear.

Marin said slowly, consciously fighting his inner tension, 'I believe a further examination should be made of the Trask case, and indeed I believe that an acquittal could be justified.'

'On what grounds?' That was Podrage. He seemed curious rather than antagonistic.

Marin made his points, one by one: 'When I read the actual treasonable statements which Trask was accused of making – and which he admitted – I found that they consisted in essence of the following: the group-free-enterprise idea needs further development. When I consider how often we've discussed that here, how often we've wondered how some particular incorrigibility of human nature might be resolved by a modification of the group idea, I can't agree that the charge against Trask justifies his death.'

Marin finished firmly: 'I believe that Wade Trask is at the beginning of a scientific career that will bring honor to the system that has made it possible. I therefore request that the verdict of guilty be altered to read: "The judge, the jury and the prosecuting staff are commended for zeal. The prisoner is censured and released for good works." '

He had become increasingly aware, as he talked, that some of those present were frowning. He saw also that he was not the only one who noticed that his arguments were having effect. Medellin glanced around the conference table, and a tremor of anxiety made a quirk in his face. Hastily, he nodded at the clerk near him. 'Will you read out the exact treasonable words uttered by Trask?'

The secretary went through his papers and presently folded

8

back several sheets of a manuscript, and in a dry voice said, 'I will now quote the words of Wade Trask, as witnesses reported against him, and according to his own admission correctly stated: "The group idea – " Mr. Trask speaking, gentlemen – "has been carried too far. My own discoveries have established the fact that social relationships require a group approach different from anything that has been attempted so far." '

Under his breath, David Marin silently cursed the madness that had made Trask forget the limitations of free speech imposed upon citizens. According to the scientist, it had happened on the day he had succeeded in transferring the nervous impulses of a chicken into the nervous system of a dog, and he had been in a state of excitement unusual for him. At the trial Trask had attempted to introduce the discovery as evidence that he was in an abnormal state of mind, but the explanation had been brushed aside.

Medellin was addressing the clerk again: 'Has the Great Judge seen these records of the trial?'

Marin felt a chill. There was a deliberateness about the way Medellin had asked the question that indicated that the Great Judge had interested himself in the Trask case.

The clerk said, 'Yes, sir. He asked for this material last week and returned it this morning.'

'Did the Great Judge,' Medellin asked, 'make any mention as to what disposition should be made of the accused?'

It was like listening to a catechism. Medellin had obviously known all along that the Great Judge had already rendered judgment.

The clerk turned several pages, as if searching, and read:

' "A clear case of treason." '

'Did he sign that?'

'He initialed it, sir.'

Death.

Marin did not ask why this prejudgment had not been introduced earlier in the proceedings. It was an outwardly preserved fiction of the council that the Great Judge did not interfere in the deliberations.

Somberly, he guessed that the mere idea of a scientist's being critical had disturbed the man who ruled the Earth of 2140 A.D.

Marin bit his lip, shook his head, and forced a twist of a smile on his face. He grew aware that routine matters in connection with the judgment were being attended to in the usual forceful fashion.

Medellin was speaking into a phone: 'You are Tilden Arallo, leader of Group 814?'

The answer came from a conference speaker. 'Tilden Arallo speaking.' It was a baritone voice, and the man must have already suspected that he was being contacted from high places, for his tone was respectful.

'This is Medellin, Chairman of the Council of Group Masters.'

'*Yes*, your excellency?'

'I have been instructed by the council to contact you in connection with your group member, Wade Trask.'

'What are the instructions?'

'The punishment for Wade Trask,' said Medellin, 'has been adjudicated as death. Accordingly, your group becomes forthwith responsible for the actions of the said Wade Trask, it being understood that no limitations except those legally permissible can be placed upon the said Wade Trask's movements and activities. The condemned seditionist, Wade Trask, shall be instructed to report to the converter for execution not later than midnight a week from this day.'

'Acknowledged,' said the voice of Tilden Arallo, 'at 10.30 A.M., August 26, 2140 A.D., on behalf of Group 814.'

'Acknowledgment recorded,' said Medellin.

The connection was broken.

Medellin glanced along the table, his gaunt face bland, his gaze bleak. He ran the bony fingers of one hand restlessly through his graying hair. 'Well, sirs,' he said, 'I believe that concludes our council business for this week. David –' he looked directly at Martin '– I want to talk to you for a few moments.'

'Yes, sir,' said Marin respectfully, but without interest. He could guess that it was about the forthcoming military operation against the 'bandit' Jorgian Queen. He was thinking that it was he who should inform Trask of the verdict.

They walked over to a corner of the council room. Medellin said in a low voice, 'David, if I had suspected that you planned a special request on Trask, I'd have warned you.' He broke off. 'But never mind that. His excellency the Great Judge and I had a discussion, and he has issued the following instructions. You will go to Camp A on the Jorgian border tomorrow, after first having lunch with the Great Judge. Take-off time is 2.00 P.M. Shortly after your arrival at Camp A you will address an audience of Jorgian revolutionaries. There will then be a two-day wait while the revolutionaries return into Jorgia. At the proper moment, those assigned the role of assassin will murder key officials of the Jorgian regime. Simultaneously, your armies will cross the border and capture the country. The Queen and her family are not to be "killed".'

Medellin paused, frowned. 'We want you to sleep with her, David. We gather she's not the world's greatest beauty, but you must give her the feeling that you personally are letting her survive because of a sudden love fancy. Pay no attention to her objections. Have her brought to your quarters, rape her if necessary, promise her your personal protection, and assure her that you will see to it that her family retains power.'

Marin nodded. He felt vaguely cynical, but not decisively so. It was not the first time that he had apparently upheld the legitimate government while in actuality seizing the country. He said, 'Who is to be informed of the date of attack?'

'No one. At this moment, only Slater and you and I and of course his excellency know this data. Employ the usual confusing tactics. Good luck.'

He walked off rapidly. Feeling singularly blank, Marin left the council room.

CHAPTER TWO

Marin waited near the parapet of the Group Central building for his hopjet to be brought to him. The air was fresh and cool; the day promised to be delightful. He noted the fact and then dismissed it from his mind. There was a tight feeling in his stomach. He wondered, a little blankly, just how he would tell Wade Trask what had happened.

Marin pursed his lips decisively. There was no doubt but that he should be the one who did the telling. He could reassure the doomed man that he would continue to do everything in his power to reverse the verdict.

Marin's thought paused at that point. His hopjet was gliding up the ramp toward him. He watched it with an almost boyish fascination in the sheer machine beauty of it. The feeling included the awareness of its silent magnetic motor, which he could not see, as well as enjoyment of its gleaming metal lines. The hopjet had stubby wings, which were not used for lift but were useful in preventing roll. The power that derived from the Earth's vast magnetic field was unconcerned with whether a man flew head down or head up. The small wings and the smaller tail kept flight sensible.

The mechanic who had brought it from some cavernous area within the building climbed out, and Marin climbed in. He flew up to a private ship lane, set the automatic pilot, and dialed Trask's private number.

There was a pause; then: 'Yes?' A baritone voice.

'Wade.'

'Oh, it's you, David.' The voice changed instantly, became urgent. 'What happened?'

Marin told him, then hurriedly reassured him. Then waited. He felt numbly unhappy. In his time he had issued many a death sentence himself and had ordered thousands of men to their deaths in battle. But this was different.

'*David, I must see you. Right away.*'

It was not a moment for hesitation. Here was a man who needed reassurance that his friends were still with him. 'Where?' Marin asked.

'At Trask Laboratories.'

For a fleeting instant, Marin considered that. It was not a good place to meet. Now that final judgment had been rendered, the laboratory would temporarily be taken over by the State. They would act quickly as a protective measure. The seizure would not jeopardize Trask's ownership. But David Marin should not be found there.

Marin hesitated for a moment, then dismissed the objection. It was a time for unqualified friendship. He said simply, 'I'll be there in ten minutes.'

'Good.'

There was a click as the connection was broken. Marin sat back feeling vaguely unhappy. For the first time in his career he had the disturbing conviction that he was making an error.

He dismissed the uneasy sensation finally. And he had time, then, to realize what would now happen to Wade Trask. The sentence of death would be formally delivered to him by Tilden Arallo, leader of Group 814. When that was done, Trask could theoretically spend his last week alive in any luxury he might choose. It was a point made much of by government propaganda. Civilization, it was said, had never before attained so high a level of freedom. Actually, escape was impossible. An electronic instrument was 'printed' on the muscles of one shoulder of an individual. The device could be activated by any control station, which would start a burning pain of gradually increasing intensity.

The device was selective. Every person in the Great Judge's domain had his own combination registered at Control Centre. There was a special combination for David Marin. And there was a separate combination for Wade Trask. Known only to a few, that was the secret of the Great Judge's absolute power.

Trask said, 'Sit.'

He was a tall, spare man, handsome in an intellectual way, with an odd air of determination in his manner. His eyes gleamed blue from behind his glasses. His movements were calm and not at all distracted.

He said, 'I have something to show you.'

Marin sat down in the chair indicated. He was puzzled but resigned. It seemed doubtful if anything Trask had to show mattered. He had seen this before, in condemned men – the belief that they had something of importance to offer, which would somehow be taken into account. It was disappointing that Trask had yielded to the same irrational hope. He should know that that aspect was exhausted.

Trask paused in front of him. 'David,' he said in a tense voice, 'I withheld something from you. Remember what I said about having transferred the nervous impulses of a chicken into the nervous system of a dog?'

Marin nodded, baffled. The other man's question seemed to have no relation to what had gone before.

Trask was talking again, urgently. 'That was actually long ago – more than a year. I've since carried the whole thing through far beyond that point. I've already experimented with Pripps, to the stage where I know exactly what I can do.'

There was a quality in Trask's voice that had in it the clang of power. The realization stiffened Marin in a stronger awareness: *Trask was not acting like a condemned man.*

He waited, his good will chilling. It was one thing to show friendship toward an injured friend and citizen. It was quite another to feel that he was on the verge of hearing actual seditious utterance.

Marin said sharply, 'Wade, what are you leading up to?'

The question seemed to act like a dash of cold water on the man. He stood very still for a moment. Then he smiled, hesitantly. Then he showed his teeth.

'David,' he said slowly, 'I'm in a position where I can oppose this sentence of death singlehandedly. But it would be much simpler if I could convince you, and so gain your co-operative assistance.'

The fateful words were spoken. In a tense amazement, Marin realized they had been implicit in Trask's actions from the first moment. It didn't even matter whether or not the other's claim was true. '*I am in a position where I can oppose this sentence of death singlehandedly.*' There it was, unmistakably.

The intent of treason . . .

He was suddenly sad, conscious of the curse of the incorrigibility of man. After three atomic wars, this kind of language was still being talked. Marin gazed gloomily at the floor; his thoughts went back over the history of Trask's trial, and he realized that it was he who had been blind, not the others.

The Great Judge had sensed this sedition in one sweep of insight and had delivered his verdict of death succinctly, with the finality of clear judgment.

Sitting there, Marin felt the hardness come into his own mind. He looked up at Trask, and he was friend no longer. But there was another thought in him, also woefully late: *Danger!*

Trask was a precisionist. He wouldn't have risked giving out this information without being prepared to deal with the consequences of a refusal.

He saw that Trask was standing, one hand in his pocket. The pocket bulged slightly. A weapon?

As their gazes met, the older man said slowly, 'I had to ask you, David, in view of our past association. You realize that.'

Marin, trying to gain time now, and an opportunity to reach for his own gun, said, 'How would I co-operate with you?'

Trask shook his head, a twisted smile on his face. 'David, I guess this has been too big a switch for you to make. I saw the look that came into your face, so I can't accept that you're considering my offer.'

His smile faded. He drew his hand out of his pocket and pointed a gas gun at Marin. 'Move over there!' he said curtly. He indicated an array of instruments in a corner of the room.

Marin climbed to his feet and walked over without a word. He waited, cool, and curious, and resigned to – what? He wasn't certain yet. There didn't seem to be death here. He looked up. His eyes met Trask's gaze.

It was Trask who looked away finally, and said, 'I'm assuming you'd like to know the details of what I'm planning.'

Marin sighed and shook his head. Men were always offering elaborate justifications for their villainous intentions. And now that he had withdrawn his good will, he was totally uninterested.

'Spare me the nonsense!' he said.

Trask hesitated. There was color in his cheeks, whether of anger or impatience, Marin couldn't decide. But when the man finally spoke he was calm again. 'Perhaps I waited too long before acting,' he said. 'I can see that you have too far to go, mentally, for me to tell you my motives. It shakes me a little, though, to realize that an experiment in political economy can have so great a hold on a man like you. So I'll just say that the group-free-enterprise idea is as hopeless for man as the group by itself, and *laissez faire* by itself. It will have to be propped up by the usual legal chicanery and will eventually fall apart when the successors of the Great Judge start quarreling among themselves.'

'You'll change all that?' Marin said.

There must have been hostility in his voice, for the flush on Trask's face grew bright. He laughed curtly, and said, 'All right, my friend, you'll learn best, anyway, from the thing itself. When you wake up, go to my apartment and carry on till you hear from me. I won't leave you in this predicament.'

It was the memory of that remark that saved Marin's sanity when he woke up.

CHAPTER THREE

Marin awakened as from a half-forgotten dream.

It was a dream that tantalized him with a sense of familiar things. And yet, it was as if he had been to many strange places and had seen and heard things that did not belong in his own life. He came weaving out of the darkness of his sleep, without fear or anxiety, and without immediate memory of what had made him unconscious.

He opened his eyes and saw that he was lying on a cot in a corner of the room where he had met Trask. There was no sign of Trask, and that brought a strong sense of relief. He closed his eyes again, stretched, yawned lazily, and finally thought, As soon as I change bodies, I'll take this equipment over to Marin's office. It shouldn't take more than a day or so after that to get to see the Great Judge.

He had the thought so naturally that several moments went by before it seemed odd and astonishing. Dumbfounded, he thought, As soon as I change *what*!

It made him sleepy to think about it. He shook his head wryly at the way a dream had pursued him into wakefulness. He recalled the dream again and was surprised to realize that he remembered everything quite clearly. There were snatches of conversation that were not out of any event that he had ever been involved in. Yet the events themselves were prosaic enough: Men earnestly discussing plans. Himself walking along streets with other people. Open prairie. Towns and cities seen from the air. A stretch of meadow, with a smiling woman coming toward him across the grass.

It was no woman that he had ever seen. These were not his memories. But they had the inner feel of things that had actually happened somewhere. It was hard to think about; he was quite sleepy now, almost dopey. And yet, with it all, he was unhappy and strangely uneasy physically.

He thought sharply, Where's Trask?

Almost immediately his attention wandered into a world of mental pictures. They were like the pictures he had already had, but now it struck him that they depicted the life of Wade Trask – an intent, frightened boy, whose fears hardened into hidden ideals, which in turn motivated a strong power drive. There was one scene, sharply defined. He was kneeling or, rather, he knelt beside a bed on which lay a dying man. And he had the feeling that this was an experiment. To the ill man, he said, 'All you have to do is ask, and then look, and then we'll do what you tell us.'

The man on the bed glared at him balefully. 'You scoundrel! You have the knowledge. Help me!'

Whoever he was in the dream spoke again. 'Don't let fear drive away your good sense. Tell me why you're sick; then tell me what to do.'

The dying man moaned. 'But that's what doctors are for. How would I know why I'm sick?'

And Trask said, 'Tell me – or die.'

That scene faded like a wisp of fog. There was no continuity in it, or in what followed – only little scenes, scattered and disconnected. It was impossible to decide just when Trask had come upon the line of inquiry that had led to his great discovery. But the end result was definite. After an initial period of settling out, the interchanged mind-force gained complete control, and all of the invaded body's memory was suppressed.

Except for having the body of another person, the interchanged 'mind' was wholly itself, with its own memories, feelings and purposes. To explain so phenomenal a transference, Trask had devised a new theory of life.

Marin was about to consider the theory which was already vaguely presenting itself when, suddenly, he understood what had happened to him. Lying there he knew the truth. It was not a half-formed thought or a suspicion. It was a burst of total understanding.

One moment he was involved with odd pieces of fears, wonders, doubts and facts, almost as if they did not apply to him. The next they simply flowed into a unit of wholeness.

What was it Trask had said? ... *transferred the nervous impulses of a chicken into the nervous system of a dog.*

He had not, until this immensely rational moment, grasped the enormousness of that discovery. If a chicken, why not a human being? Why not the nervous impulses of Trask into the nervous system of Marin?

And Marin into Trask.

I am lying here, thought Group Master David Marin numbly. And it is I and my memories, but the body of Wade Trask. And he is out there with his memories and his purposes, and he looks like me. To all outward purpose, he is me. If he is bold enough, he can go anywhere. He can even get in to see the Great Judge.

He remembered Trask's confidence, and he did not doubt but that the man would be bold enough. He opened his eyes again as the realization struck him. Now, automatically, he climbed to his feet.

Not until the action was completed did he realize that he had functioned easily in Trask's body. In a single, continuous motion he had used the other man's hands, his feet, his muscles and his senses.

The sharp awareness made him look down, made him bring up his arms, so that, for the first time, he could look at ... himself.

There was no conscious thought behind what he did then. He started to run.

Outside, he saw that his hopjet was not in the laboratory parking lot. He paused, but only momentarily, and did not come to a final stop until he reached a Taxi-Air stand. Breathless, he waited. Still breathless, a few minutes later, he gave Trask's apartment address to the driver and settled into a seat.

Apathy.

He sat there, and his sense of loss was so great that there seemed no meaning to what he was doing. He was nothing. He was an area of black grief in space-time. A man who had lost his own identity. In a kind of agony, he reached up and fingered Trask's glasses; he who had had an eagle's vision. He recalled how quickly he had tired while running and how long he had remained tired. The iron-hard body of David Marin was a tireless machine by comparison.

He stirred finally and looked down through the transparent glass at the city. He thought, then, Where am I going?

And then he thought, Why, of course, Trask's apartment. That's where he told me to go.

He sat for a time, numb again, accepting that Trask's home was a logical destination for the person who looked like Wade Trask.

'We've landed, sir,' said the voice of the driver from the speaker beside him.

'Landed?' Marin looked up.

Marin started to get up, started to accept that he would do exactly as Trask had suggested. Then he scowled and sat down again.

'I've changed my mind,' he said. 'Take me to—' He named a park in the center of the city.

It was a beauty spot that he, as Marin, had often gone to, to resolve problems of military strategy.

As the Taxi-Air took off, Marin drew a deep breath into the shallow lungs of Wade Trask.

He had a problem such as no man in all the world had ever faced before.

Having arrived at the park, he sat down on a bench. It was still morning, although the sun leaned toward noon. He felt tiny mental shocks every little while as he realized that so little time had actually gone by.

A dozen times he turned his attention to his problem and instantly backed away, instantly blanked out on it. Restlessly, aimlessly, he kicked at the walk with the toe of his boot. Restlessly, unhappily, he walked along one path, then another, then back to his bench, only to get up again, walk again, sit again, and walk.

CHAPTER FOUR

It was a few minutes before ten o'clock that night when Marin, worn-out and gloomy, opened the door of Trask's apartment and entered a spacious living room. It had finally dawned on him that his only solution was to find Trask again.

A thin, dark-haired young woman sprang up from a couch and ran toward him. She flung her arms around his neck and, before he could decide to resist, planted a kiss on his lips.

Marin pulled away. The young woman drew back, pouting. 'I'm here for you,' she said. 'As soon as your group heard that you had been sentenced, they hired me and sent me over.'

Marin said, 'Oh!' And he was briefly, profoundly, interested. A bought woman for a man who could probably no longer obtain the favors of a woman who was free. It was a control method, and the speed with which the group leaders had acted indicated how practical a method it must be for dealing with a condemned person.

Marin studied the woman curiously. She was slim, and bright, and evidently thought well of herself, for there was a pertness to her manner which was appealing. Marin released himself from her grasp and glanced round a room that was as luxuriously appointed as any he had ever seen. Paneled oak walls, high ceiling, a plastic window that – except for the alcove at either end – extended from wall to wall and from floor to ceiling.

Involuntarily, Marin's gaze jumped to the right wall. A large clock stood there, built into one of the panels. It stirred a memory – not his own memory, but the Trask body-brain recalling that the clock concealed one entrance to Trask's apartment laboratory, a secret place where Trask had made many of his experiments. The other entrance was in the den.

The casual thought came also that the clock itself was one of the old outlets of the Brain.

The Brain had disappeared during the war, leaving only such reminders of its existence as this clock. And most such remnants had been destroyed or had fallen into disuse.

Marin noted that the clock hands showed exactly the same

time as his watch, a few seconds before ten. He was about to turn away when the instrument gave an arresting clang.

There was a pregnant pause, with a faint undercurrent of sound from the interior of the clock. Then a musical chime sounded. Simultaneously, colored lights played across the screen on the clock face. The echoing sound of the chime faded, and there was another pause. Drums began to throb. They receded into the background, and a man's baritone voice pronounced in the well-known spoken Model English of mechanical voices that 'It be now 10.00 P.M. for August 26, 2140 A.D.' There was another pause, and then the same voice stated that the weather 'did be' cool for August, and the sky 'did be a little clouded.'

There was a clash of cymbals followed by the same bell-like clang which had introduced the entire elaborate ritual. Then silence.

Marin, who had listened and watched with total interest, grew aware that the woman was gazing at him. She seemed slightly puzzled, and it struck him that Wade Trask would scarcely have noticed the clock; it must be completely familiar to him.

Standing there, he pretended to be in deep thought. He looked up. 'What do you do?' he asked. 'Sleep with dead men?'

She seemed to shrivel a little, but she said nothing. Marin, who was not really critical, nevertheless persisted: 'What are your rates?'

She was calm again. 'From a hundred to five hundred a week.'

For the first time it occurred to Marin that he was not just trying to distract her attention from his preoccupation with the clock. He was seriously considering taking her on. And that was a milestone idea indeed. All in a flash his mind went back to Delindy Darrell, the most beautiful woman who had ever borne him children. They had lived together for nearly three years. But for six months now she had been the mistress of the Great Judge.

The whole half year since, he had been without interest in women.

He said, with sudden gentleness, 'My dear, you may stay if

21

you wish, but the fact is I don't feel very sincere.' He smiled, and added, with a sardonic note in his voice, 'I'll consider you a five-hundred-dollar girl.'

She laughed, came over to him lightly, kissed him, hugged him – one quick squeeze – and then, head flung back, walked into the bedroom.

Marin sat down in a chair facing the door, and for the first time that day it occurred to him as a solid possibility that there were many things he could have done. For all he knew, Trask had long since used his resemblance to David Marin to seek an audience with the Great Judge. *For all he knew,* Trask had already forced an identity shift with the dictator.

I should have done something! Marin thought, pale and shaken.

The intense feeling of anxiety passed. Obviously, there was nothing he could have done – or he would have done it. The fact that he was now emerging from the shock effect of what had happened was to his credit. Surely, it was the greatest shock any human being anywhere had ever had.

Tomorrow, he thought finally – that was shortly before midnight – I'll act.

If it wasn't already too late.

Wearily, still conscious of the immense strain of that day, Marin headed for the bedroom. He stopped short just inside the door. Because he had forgotten the woman.

She lay in one of the beds. There was a glint of bare shoulder above the sheets; and she turned lazily, looked at him, and said, 'In case you've even thought about it, my name is Riva Allen.'

Marin walked over and sat down on the bed beside her. Mention of her name did remind him of something else. It had been his understanding that group living had eliminated the woman of the streets. And yet here was one, and a very engaging one at that. What was more, she had been sent *by* a group. It was an unsuspected seamy side to his picture of life under the Great Judge, and he was briefly curious.

'Tell me about yourself, your early life.'

It was an indirect way of asking how she had become what she was – designed to by-pass her defenses. It seemed to slip by them.

'I was born,' she began, 'in the community that looked after the Brain.' Then she added, 'That's why I was interested in that clock of yours out there. First one I've seen in a long time.'

Marin said, 'The Brain!'

She seemed not to notice the odd tone of his voice, for she went on quietly, 'That's why I could never get a number. They won't register anyone who was at any time connected with the Brain before it disappeared.' She broke off. 'Where did you get that clock?'

Marin scarcely heard. 'You're not registered!' he said. But the words were not a true reaction. He was thinking: The Control is still paying *that* much attention to the Brain. And that was indeed a mighty idea, brand-new for him. To cover the impact of it, he said, 'How do you live and eat?'

'I have a temporary food card, which is renewed every six months.'

'But where do you live?' he asked.

'Here,' she said.

Marin was impatient. 'But that's this week. You must have a permanent—' He stopped; then, gently, 'Where do you keep your clothes?'

'In a locker at the air station. It costs twenty-five cents a day. There's a bathroom upstairs, and I change there.'

He was a man who had his own urgent problems, but he visualized the life of this rejected girl, and it hurt him. She seemed to be full of energy, and – despite her deadly existence – operating on a high level of liveliness and good spirits. He began to question her casually. What kind of job had she held? Where did she sleep when she didn't have a Wade Trask to provide a temporary haven for her? What about mail? Had she ever tried living in the Pripp section of the city? What about moving to the country? ... It was a long list of questions. Riva replied, sometimes vaguely, but she seldom hesitated. In about an hour he had her life in outline.

Her early childhood was dim. She had recollections of being with parents who moved, drove, flew – always seeking remoter distances of escape. And always the reaching red tape of the Great Judge's registrars followed them. They were among the minority who were invariably refused group status. Their past connection with the Brain dogged them, brought them to ruin and hopelessness. The finale came with crushing unexpectedness. The Control descended one day upon the hovel where they lived. The father, unbelieving and protesting, was led out and put against the wall of the shack, and shot. There was no explanation, no further direct interference – but the bread-winner was gone. For mother and daughter, the time of nightmare had come.

The transition to woman of the town took place in direct proportion to the need for food.

Riva was beginning to show marked signs of sleepiness, and so Marin asked his key question in as conversational a tone as he could manage. 'But where did the Brain go?'

'It flew off in a spaceship.'

'In a *what*?'

'Spaceship – you know, space, the moon, Venus, Mars.'

'But that's just a myth,' Marin protested. 'There's some mention of space flight before the second atomic war, but it's pretty generally conceded that . . .' His voice trailed off. He realized he was talking to a woman who was sound asleep.

Marin undressed and slipped into the second bed. He lay there wide awake, thinking tensely, The Brain must still be . . . alive.

Nothing else could explain the tremendous effort the Judge's men had made to stamp out all those who had ever been connected with it.

He recalled something he had once heard: that the Brain had made the Great Judge immortal. At the time he had merely shrugged. Although it had been going on for years, he had always regarded references to the immortality of the dictator as a particularly childish form of propaganda. Yet somewhere here was a fearful reality, or Riva Allen would not be in her present plight. Hers was a small story, but it gave substance to all the things he had ever heard about the Brain.

His mind drifted oddly . . .

. . . Hard to imagine what moment would be right for a rebellion against so powerful an adversary as an immortal dictator. The group in Jorgia might delay *their* action too long; he couldn't wait.

Marin frowned sleepily. 'Did I think that?' He had not ever before even considered rebellion. And what was that about a Jorgian group? Could it be that, just for an instant, here at the

24

edge of sleep, a Trask plan had slipped through to his consciousness?

But why rebellion? It didn't fit. A man who could shift his awareness and his identity from one body to another didn't need revolutions. Besides, it would be impossible.

The group idea, combined with free enterprise, and pregnant with great ideas, was just beginning to take hold. Like a giant, it strode over the land, crushing all resistance and simultaneously inspiring hope. At such moments men did not listen easily to voices that warned against faraway disaster or urged the possibility of even greater creativity.

Again his mind wandered. If they don't act, he thought, I'll have to act on my own.

He felt relieved that he hadn't told anyone of his invention. And so, all by himself, he was able to act – on the greatest scale.

Marin slept uneasily, and his dreams were vague yet purposeful. He seemed to be permeated with secret plans that were not his own.

CHAPTER FIVE

Marin awoke with his whole body tingling. It was instantly so strange a feeling that he held himself very still, inwardly shaking with anxiety.

He grew acutely aware of how dark it was, and an ancient, primeval fear of the night stole over his body. He listened, straining for a sound. It seemed to him that only an unusual noise would have brought him to such a tense alertness. The prickly feeling in his skin grew stronger instead of fading; it was not a pleasant sensation.

Astoundingly, then, he had a sense of death so strong that the fear in him made an icy flow along his spine. With a terrified intensity, he forced his neck to unbend, and he lifted his head and peered toward the door.

And then, he felt blank.

Lines of a luminescent something extended through the door of the bedroom half-way to his bed. As he watched, rigid and unbelieving, the forward ends lashed out and moved to within inches of the bed. All the lines – and there were scores of them – crinkled and glittered as that movement occurred.

Marin slipped out of the bed. It was a sideways action, a rolling motion, so swiftly achieved that he was on the floor before he realized that, except for a faint rustling of the sheets, he had gotten out from under without a sound.

He had time for a quick glance at the other bed. The soft sound of breathing came from it. Clearly, Riva was unaware of what was happening.

Thought of her receded into the background of his mind, for at that instant the luminous lines reared into view as if being thrown, and fell across his bed. One of the ends seemed almost to brush his face as it whipped past. It fell, however, and dangled against the sheet like a rope.

It was the automaton characteristic that ended Marin's retreat. He climbed jerkily to his feet, took several backward steps, and then, all in one leap of comprehension, he took control of what was happening.

This was a mechanical device. Weird, even incredible – but a machine, not a life form. With the element of surprise gone, its danger to him consisted wholly in the mystery of it – and from whomever was directing it.

He reached back to the clothes rack, where his coat hung, and pulled it free, softly, gingerly. From the right-hand pocket, he drew his gas gun. In the darkness, he lowered the coat to the floor. Then, clutching the gun, he moved around the bed. He felt free of fear, but caution still rode high inside him.

He reached the door, and that brought the crisis in his caution. Go through, or look? Step over the lines, or – what?

He looked. He peered gingerly around the doorjamb. As he saw where the luminosity came from, he sighed, and thought, Why, of course!

The radiance was strung out from one of the 'outlets' of the clock. Marin made a calculation, then jumped through the door, over the lines. He walked hurriedly to the clock and quickly searched for an electrical connection that he could turn off.

He found a switch that said, *on*, and pushed it to *off*. The lines, as far as he could see them to the doorway of the bedroom, vanished instantly. The illuminated face of the clock darkened. He pushed the switch again – *on*. The clock face lighted, but there was no sign of the silvery bright lines.

Marin walked to the bedroom door. A quick glance through verified that the long strings of light were gone from there also and that the fantastic episode was temporarily over.

Gently he drew the door shut, waited silently for many seconds to make sure Riva had not wakened, and then switched on the lights of the big room.

One thing astonished him. The attack, if that was what it was, had been aimed at him – or, rather, at Wade Trask.

Marin's thought poised there. There was another possibility: *by* Trask, not *at* Trask.

Deliberately, with that idea in mind, he stood and looked the room over. He was remembering the thought he had had when he first entered the apartment earlier – about the hidden laboratory. Oddly, *then* he had known with casual certainty exactly how to get into it. Now it was a vague memory only – something to do with the clock.

He opened the secret door five minutes later and, entering, found himself in a long narrow room. It was brightly lighted. He wondered if his action of opening the door had automatically switched on the lights. His gaze flicked past the paraphernalia of an electronic engineer – motors, metal panels with dials and meters and switches. There were a number of large instruments suspended from the ceiling, and one entire wall resembled the switchboard of an automatic telephone exchange. There were several boxes in one corner, and on the floor at the end of the table . . .

Marin grabbed his gas gun and froze.

Slowly he permitted his tensed fingers to relax from the metal stock of the weapon. He walked carefully forward and knelt beside the limp body of a man that lay there, face downward. It was a familiar-looking form; and even as he noticed that it was still breathing; even as he reached down and laboriously in that confined space turned it over, the feeling of recognition grew stronger.

The feeling was still there presently as he gazed down at the upturned face. It was quite familiar, but after several seconds his heart sank. He had no idea who it was.

He stood up and looked around for cord. He found thin electric wire in a drawer of the table. Skillfully, swiftly, he bound the man's hands and feet in such a way as not to cut off circulation.

Ought to be awake by morning, he thought. He can do his explaining then.

The man had a look of having been shot by a gas gun. Since it required elaborate equipment to determine which gas, it was better not to try antidotes but simply to let a natural awakening occur.

Marin stepped out of the laboratory presently, carefully drew the clock back into position, and then considered what his next move should be.

Sleep, of course.

He returned to the bedroom, closing the door this time. Although actually he doubted if what had happened would now be repeated.

A Trask agent had come into the place, and somehow what he had tried to do had backfired. The fact that Trask had sent an agent at all in such a peculiar fashion would have to be explained – in the morning.

In the darkness, Marin crawled back into bed. He felt tired now, and there was a keyed-up feeling in his stomach. I'm missing something, he thought tensely.

What could it possibly be?

He slept on that for about an hour. And woke up, and thought, Why, of course. I didn't use Trask's glasses when I jumped out of bed earlier; and yet I could see perfectly.

He should have known that that would happen. The armed forces, with their elaborate methods of disguising their agents, had discovered that changes in perception could be produced by various manipulations.

His life-force, with his attitudes, had been in control of Trask's body for several hours. He must already have altered the entire body 'tone', in spite of his depression.

He thought about that for a long while, and then the uneasiness came back. Because vision wasn't what was bothering him. It was something else.

What? ...

He slept. And woke up. And thought, My God, that man is ...

David Marin!

CHAPTER SIX

The phone rang.

One by one the hard, tense speculations fell away from Marin. In an instant they were gone, and he opened his eyes.

It was broad daylight, which startled him. He had had the impression that he had spent the night thinking of a score of things he must do. There was the body of . . . himself . . . in the hidden laboratory. There was the fact that he had to fly to Asia at 2.00 P.M. There was his feeling that he could not afford to give time to any activity in his capacity as a Group Master. In that connection, he had speculated widely as to the best way to avoid doing so. And there was the Brain; he must investigate that. Anything that was the object of so much fearful activity by the Great Judge could be useful. Delindy, the war in Asia and Trask's invention had likewise – so it seemed to him – engaged his attention. But evidently he had been sleeping, not thinking. At least, not consciously thinking. He smiled ruefully and reached for the phone. And then once more he hesitated.

Suppose this were someone he did not know who would take past association for granted.

The phone rang again while he braced himself to meet such a situation. Then he picked up the receiver.

A man's voice said, 'Ralph Scudder, Mr Trask.'

Marin suppressed an exclamation of recognition. He knew of this man – or, rather, Pripp. Ralph Scudder, Pripp leader – which meant gang leader. Scudder was known to be the head of Pleasure, Incorporated, a semi-secret Pripp organization which controlled gambling and prostitution – by Pripp women – and engaged in innumerable petty crimes. It was believed among Control officers that the organization was protected by the Great Judge.

Marin drew a slow, deep breath. 'Yes?' he said.

'I've got a meeting set up for what you and I talked about – 10.00 P.M. tonight.'

Marin had a feeling of inner contraction. 'Where?' he asked.

'Call "Pleasure" before you come. They'll direct you.'

29

'I'll be there,' said Marin.

He hung up, without waiting to discover if Scudder had anything more to say.

He felt relieved. He had got off lightly on his first Trask contact. If it was Trask there in the laboratory, then he could learn from him what the two – the scientist and the Pripp – had talked about.

As his thought reached that point, his glance fell on the adjoining bed. It was neatly made, and unoccupied. Marin studied it soberly and finally shrugged. He had neither the right nor the desire to control Riva Allen's movements. But it was odd, and quite unnecessary, that she should have departed so silently. Presently he felt irritated by it also. For – just like that – erotic need touched him, an almost atavastic desire flickering in his cells, needing satiation.

The flame of his desire dimmed. He grew more aware of how much he had changed from the evening before. The heavy sense of loss was gone out of him, almost as if a weight had lifted – slightly. He could see not one but several solutions to his problem.

Warn the Great Judge, if necessary. Surprisingly, that could be an answer, simple, straightforward. But, first, there were a few things to find out. For example, he should wait until the body in the laboratory returned to consciousness. It just might not be Trask.

He lay back, in genuine awe at the possibility. What a fantastic discovery Trask had made. In a single comprehensive act of genius, he had upset the balance of power. All the war machines of the armed forces, all the cunning of an Edmund Slater, was by-passed by a purely mechanical means of altering the identity of bodies. Like some demon out of antiquity, the man who controlled such a device could 'possess' human beings and *be* them, one at a time.

And since men would not easily grasp the danger, a determined Trask could strike at the very top of the power group of a planet-wide government – except for one thing.

There he lay in his own laboratory, a prisoner, victim, of some petty disaster – perhaps awake now, considering the extent of the catastrophe.

Marin felt weary. But the idea of talking to Trask was motivation enough to send him into the laboratory.

. . . His body lay there, limp, breathing, unconscious.

CHAPTER SEVEN

He returned to bed, and slept.

And awoke to the sound of the bedroom door opening. Riva Allen walked in. She was fully dressed and was carrying two suitcases, which, on one level of logic, instantly explained her absence. She seemed very smart and good looking in a bluish suit, and very contrite in the way she shook her head and said, 'Oh, I woke you up.'

Marin said, 'It's all right. It's time.'

He glanced at his watch and sighed. Twenty to nine. Time indeed for him to be up. As he swung to the edge of the bed, Riva walked past him and set the bags down. She said unnecessarily, 'I got my things.'

Marin mentally visualized her getting her belongings from the air station, winced, and muttered, 'Good. Make yourself at home.'

The girl was regarding him with an annoyed smile. She said, 'There's really very little point in my staying if you don't take any more advantage of my presence than you did last night.'

Her obvious irritation put Marin in good humor again. 'I was in apathy,' he said. 'It won't happen again.' He stood up and patted her cheek. She caught his hand and swung toward him with a sensuous movement of her body. He held her briefly and then murmured something about going out. And when she still held on to him, he said, 'Tonight!' and released himself.

In the bathroom, he made his plans for the day.

I'll disguise myself as Marin, he thought. Then he paused, shocked to realize how casually he had considered that. Not that it would be hard. The armed forces had developed the science of disguise to such an ultimate point that, given two individuals who were not too different physically, virtual duplication was possible.

Marin smiled into the mirror with his thin Trask face. He was certainly the only person who would find it easy to play to perfection the role of David Marin, Group Master. But that would be only the beginning.

He was a man who had many things to do, and he wasn't sure as yet how to do them. His first task was, of course, to carry out his immediate military tasks. But he could return by this evening from his first trip to Jorgia. Once the battle started two days hence, it would be more difficult to get away.

Nevertheless, if everything worked out correctly, he might be able to avoid the need to explain the incredible thing that had happened. His task: Somehow to switch Trask and Marin back to their proper states. Then, truly himself again, he would be in full control, able to discuss the invention realistically and deal with all problems. Afterward, he could justify any action he might now take.

Fully dressed, Marin went up to the roof. He felt profound relief and satisfaction as he saw that his own hopjet was parked in the visitors' section. Its presence was a kind of solidified proof that it was actually Trask back there in the laboratory. In a few minutes, with the equipment he had aboard, he would be on the way to achieving his immediate purposes.

He hurried into the machine and climbed rapidly to the private plane lane – and set the controls on automatic flight.

CHAPTER EIGHT

The hopjet's equipment for creating disguises was the standard kit used by the armed forces. Even so, it took a little while. The first part of the task consisted of 'printing' a series of simple electronic circuits on the muscles of the face, head and neck, just under the skin. This was done by a high-velocity gas-gun device which projected a special gas through a mold and therefore in a pattern and at such speed that the skin was not broken.

Marin waited for the gas to assume its flexible but tough circuit form. Then he switched the power on the control kit and began to manipulate the dials, one for each circuit. Each time he turned a knob a series of muscles tightened or relaxed. The muscles affected were a key to the shape of the face.

After his experience of the previous night, Marin did not trust his memory of his own appearance. He used as a model the photograph of himself behind the sealed, transparent identification plate on the hopjet's control panel. As he manipulated the dials, first the expression and then the appearance of Trask's face altered.

Presently, he had the best approximation he could get of David Marin. Satisfied, he closed a master switch and established a 'set'.

The next stage was a refinement of the earlier ones. He 'printed' circuits on key voice muscles and subtly adjusted the tensions in them until the voice of Wade Trask sounded like a taped recording of David Marin's voice on the plane's phone answering system.

He tried on, one after the other, several of his own suits from the hopjet's clothes locker. Two, one dark, one light, fitted reasonably well, the others being too full across the chest and shoulders.

Marin chose the lighter of the two; and that also was out of long experience. For any color or brightness attracted attention away from the individual, even as it seemed to add to his personality.

A few minutes later he landed on the roof of the Group Masters building – and was committed to the impersonation of . . . himself.

CHAPTER NINE

He found the Control Chief in a large office which was bare of ornamentation except for a large steel desk and several chairs. The walls of the office were of concrete, as was the floor; and there were no instruments – which was wryly amusing to Marin, who knew how much mechanization this lean, restless, determined man utilized in his murderous work. The very absence of any electronic equipment reflected perversely the other's immense respect for what such things might be used for.

It was evident, after one look at his office, that Edmund Slater, spy chief of a ruthless dictator, had no intention of being spied on in his own inner sanctum.

Slater was pacing the floor when Marin entered. He paused at the far side of the office, faced about, and smiled in a frowning way.

'David, that was an unwise thing you did yesterday at the council meeting. We're dealing with a gentleman who plays by rules that are rough yet terribly reasonable. Even I am not irreplaceable.'

Marin said, 'I presume we're talking about the Trask affair. I didn't realize I was walking into a bear trap.'

Slater shook his head. His gaze was briefly unwinking, and his eyes had a greenish color. He said, 'There's more to that affair than your not knowing the danger. It was an emotional defense you made. There was a note in your voice that I never expected to hear there. Just a touch of grief, David; and I must admit I don't understand it even now.'

He paused, and he was still unmoving; it was as if he waited for a cue from Marin that would help him to understand. Marin studied the man, and now he himself was frowning. There was pressure being applied here, and obviously he couldn't give the true answers; so each moment devoted to this line of conversation was wasted.

Marin said quietly, 'Ed, I wish you'd stop dramatizing your own fears. You must know I cannot take into account in any of my thinking the possibility that I will be suspected of having ulterior motives in my actions. If the fear that you're trying to induce in me should even touch me, then you'd better start investigating right away. Now, what's really on your mind? I also have something to discuss.'

The slim, sinister little man hesitated perceptibly. Then he laughed, not unpleasantly, and said, 'As you know, this department occasionally requests help from yours in training personnel for liaison work with you.'

Marin said, 'The arrangement is satisfactory, I hope?' He waited. Slater had obviously brought the matter up for a special reason, since it had long been handled at levels below Group Master rank.

Slater said, with a faint smile, 'I have a young fellow I want

34

you to take along this afternoon. It's his first contact with war, and, as you'll see, he needs training.'

Marin shook his head. 'I can't be bothered with that today. My schedules are too tight.'

Slater smiled again. 'The Great Judge and I,' he said, 'are particularly interested in this boy. When you see him, you might take a look at him and ask yourself if he reminds you of anyone you know.'

Marin sighed, and made a mental calculation as to when the first mating games had taken place. That was back just after the war – twenty years! This could be one of the children of the Great Judge, as a result of the mating games of those early years. The leader had participated the first few times, until the number of women offering him their tokens grew so great that it became a matter of public interest that he withdraw.

There was nothing for Marin to do but cancel his refusal. He said, 'Have him at rocket take-off at two o'clock.'

Slater nodded approvingly. Then: 'Now – what's on your mind?'

There was a long pause.

Presently, Marin climbed to his feet and walked over to the window. It was going to be harder to say than he had expected. What he wanted was so vital that he could not afford an error in his presentation. The interview had already proved more dangerous than he had anticipated.

It was natural, as he stood there looking out, that his gaze fell upon a structure that rested like a special penthouse upon the great Group Masters building. It was there, in six days, that Trask must report for execution. The main section of the protuberance was low-built, and unbeautiful in its square solidity. Barred windows gave the usual bleak, repressive appearance of a prison. At either end twin shafts of metal and concrete rose straight up several hundred feet. Here were the muffling chambers of the converters, where step by step the radioactivity of the secondary materials was either rechanneled or suppressed, or – if nothing else availed – the affected compounds were automatically packed in safe containers and removed to distant burial grounds.

From where he stood, Marin could not see the power-house

itself or the power broadcasting antennae. The former was an extension of the 'penthouse' and the latter was located in a raised section that he could not see from this window. But he knew that somewhere in the vaulted underground of this structure was the relay which – when activated – could effect a burning sensation in the shoulders of Trask's body, and so by the pain it created draw him inexorably to his doom.

Marin felt himself grow tense, and wondered how many men had considered how they might penetrate this fortress and erase their own records. He had never heard of anyone's succeeding. The realization spurred him now. He turned from the window and said, 'Ed, I'd like information on a subject that has been taboo even in the Group Masters Council.'

Slater, who had half turned away, faced about and looked up at him from narrowed eyelids. 'What subject is that?'

'The Brain.'

There was a long pause, and it seemed to Marin that the smaller man actually changed color. He seemed to shrivel a little. 'David,' he said finally, 'if I were to inform the Great Judge that you had mentioned that name, he would really begin to feel unhappy about you.'

Marin waited, not trusting himself to speak.

Edmund Slater went on in a low voice. 'I'm in charge of the ceaseless search for the Brain. My agents are men who know that it is death for them if they even tell anyone that such a search is in progress. I suggest that you forget that this conversation ever took place.'

Marin did not discount one word of the warning. But he did not hesitate. He said, 'I want to put this thought to you. If the Brain is still in existence, you *know* where it is.'

The agile mind of the slender, wiry man in front of him seemed to reach instantly to all the nuances of meaning in those words. 'So much data,' he said, and he spoke like a man who is thinking out loud. 'Tens of thousands of clues – so many pieces to fit together; maybe it needs a new, sharp mind to look at all the pictures.' His eyes lost their faraway look and focused on Marin. He seemed very tense, holding in an inner excitement. 'David,' he said, in a tone of voice as suppressed as his manner, 'I believe yours is the biggest thought that has come into this search in a decade. I'd like to have a further discussion with you before deciding whether or not I should go ahead on my own or bring the matter up to the Great Judge.'

Marin, who had time limitations, said, 'Where was the Brain last seen?'

'We have conflicting reports,' said Slater. 'The last known version was about twenty-four years ago. A tramp, now dead, made a deposition to the effect that at about 2.00 A.M. one morning he saw a giant ship hovering over the mountain inside which the Brain was housed. As he watched, the great camouflaged steel doors above opened, and the ship sank down the huge shaft, which had been constructed in that fashion so that the Brain could be removed in the event of danger. Evidently the ship had its bottom torn out, or else it was built with sliding doors that could expose almost the entire interior. Far more important, this had clearly been planned for in all construction work done to strengthen the Brain against attacks from the air. Steel outjuttings, holes drilled in the metal walls of the building, and various extruding devices whereby the whole structure could be bolted, and welded, and joined to male or female moldings in the interior of the ship, and so transported in one piece – everything had obviously been planned with mathematical accuracy. I need hardly tell you that we've tried to trace down every person associated with that flight.'

Marin recalled Riva Allen's statement about the Brain's having flown to another planet, and realized that he was being given as straightforward an account as was available. 'What did you find?' he asked.

'Hypnosis, mental control from a distance, weird use of electronic circuits directly onto the brains of human beings – we just couldn't take any chances with most of the people who were connected even indirectly. I could tell you how many people were killed, but you wouldn't like the figures. They sound unpleasant in the very total. But even as it was, we took pity on some of them, and merely keep an eye on them, or otherwise control them or their descendants.'

Marin thought of Riva, and now the picture was clear indeed. Her story and this account fitted rather well. The only thing was that she would never know how narrowly she and her mother had escaped death. It would actually have been simpler to destroy them. The number of dead must be large for two

37

men like the Great Judge and Slater to have finally paused in their executioner's role and made alleviations.

Marin said slowly, 'Do you know who was the master planner behind the Brain's escape?'

'Yes.'

'Who?'

'The Brain,' said Edmund Slater.

The barren room seemed somehow a proper setting for those words. The concrete walls and floor offered a protective barrier against all things mechanical. It was almost as if here, in this bleak chamber, and here only, a man might be safe against the cunning of an electronic brain. One might almost imagine humankind's making its last stand from a room such as this against the encroachment of the hordes controlled by a thinking machine.

For Marin, the existence of such a super-machine was a difficult concept to accept. He knew that experts had examined outlets of the Brain; and there was no doubt that they represented aspects of electronic science that had been lost and not yet reinvented. But there was an implication in Slater's words of a figure vast beyond human comprehension and – an idea even harder to grasp – interested *in* man.

He stood with his back to the window, frowned at Slater, and said, 'What does the Brain hope to achieve?'

'World dictatorship. Complete control of the human race.'

Marin started to laugh, and then he saw that Slater was serious. He stopped his laughter abruptly, and said, 'I don't know exactly why that struck me as funny. But I can't quite conceive of a machine's worrying about or caring about human beings.'

Slater shook his head. 'What we have here is not an ego but a computation, not a power-mad monster but a fine instrument that is resolving a problem which it was asked to deal with. We don't want to destroy the Brain – if we can help it; we want to regain control of it and restate the problem in less sweeping terms. Yes, we want to be rid of war, and we want a peaceful world functioning sanely – but not at the expense of human self-determinism. The Brain was instructed to do everything necessary to achieve an optimum solution to the war. Evidently it places a precise evaluation on the meaning of *optimum*.'

Marin's thought leaped back to his wonder about the propaganda that the Great Judge was immortal. It did not seem an opportune time to discuss that. He realized that he would not find all the answers here – not yet, not today; and so he glanced at his watch, saw that it was time he was on his way, and said, 'Ed, I'll see you again. But this is a strange story you've told me, and I can't believe all of it. The Brain never plotted anything, except on request. It might reason a situation and present the data for human consideration and action. But any action *it* took would be through servo-mechanisms, however refined and perceptive.'

Slater said, 'This machine is the greatest device ever evolved. It can take generalized instructions and then feed itself the necessary detailed orders, carrying them out through servo-mechanisms which it also sets up. Of course, there had to be a broad base of previous construction. But I can assure you that for a hundred years the scientific and engineering brains of the world helped it establish that base.'

Marin started for the door. Then he turned. He said abruptly, 'Do any clues point to Jorgia on the Brain?'

Slater shook his head slowly. He seemed puzzled. 'What are you getting at?'

'We're on the eve of battle,' said Marin, 'and I have a sudden feeling that there are other forces at work besides what is visible.'

'You've been right there with us at all the discussions,' said Slater.

Marin wasn't as sure of that as he would have been a few days before. He frowned thoughtfully. 'Outwardly, the scene looks the same as the others – I've got to admit that. We couldn't ask for a better setup than a royal government, complete with arch-conservative attitudes. That such a group could gain control of what for two hundred years was a Communist state was certainly one of the more bizarre results of the war.'

He shook his head irritably and concluded, 'Well, we'll knock 'em over. Good-by.' He went out, closing the door behind him.

It was time for lunch. Time to find out what the dictator was up to.

CHAPTER TEN

From his hopjet, Marin looked down upon the metropolis below. He saw the city now, not as it was but in his mind's eye: as it had been in the old films, during the great wars, smoldering and sickening in its death throes.

Twice the phoenix city had risen from the ashes, the first time taking the conventional city form, with structures shaped according to the will of each owner and streets like long arms reaching into the distances, or crisscrossing each other in a fantastic repetition. The second rebirth had taken place under the firm, guiding hand of the Great Judge; and so, the city that Marin gazed down upon was a pattern of squares. Each had its park area, but always, regardless of its size, the backbone of buildings towered high around the perimeter of each square. It was argued that an atomic bomb could be contained within a few such squares, its great dispersing power suppressed or diverted by the solidly built, towering perimeter of the affected squares.

For Marin, the city had an almost medieval look. The effect was belied by the swarms of hopjets, and Taxi-Airs, and other aircraft, large and small. But his training had sharpened his ability to shut out extraneous material and to see essentials; and so, he saw a city pattern that had a formal, old-fashioned beauty. The squares were too rigid, but their widely varying sizes provided some of the randomness so necessary to achieve what was timeless in true art. The numerous parks, perpetually green and rich with orderly growth, gave an over-all air of graceful elegance. The city of the Great Judge looked prosperous and long-enduring.

Ahead, the scene changed, darkened, became alien. The machine glided forward over a vast, low-built, rambling gray mass of suburb that steamed and smoked, and here and there hid itself in its own rancorous mists.

Pripp City!

Actually, the word was Pripps: *P*reliminary *R*estriction *I*ndicated *P*ending *P*ermanent *S*egregation. It was one of those alphabetical designations, and an emotional nightmare to have all other identification removed and to find yourself handed a card which advised officials that you were under the care of the Pripps organization. The crisis had been long ago now, more than a quarter of a century, but there was a line in fine print at the bottom of each card. A line that still made the identification a potent thing, a line that stated: *Bearer of this card is subject to the death penalty if found outside restricted area.*

In the beginning it had seemed necessary. There had been a disease, virulent and deadly, perhaps too readily and too directly attributed to radiation. The psychological effects of the desperate terror of thousands of people seemed not to have been considered as a cause. The disease swept over an apathetic world and produced merciless reaction: permanent segregation, death to transgressors, and what seemed final evidence of the rightness of what had been done: people who survived the disease ... changed.

As the hopjet landed in the square, Marin saw what was an ordinary sight in Pripp City: a man with the head of a tiger — catlike eyes, catlike ears, even the fuzz of a furry face — walked along beside a woman who showed clearly some of the characteristics of a fish. They were definitely human beings, but a ghastly hand had reached up along the genetic line and marked them. Out of a man's evolutionary history had come partial blueprints of past life-forms.

Seeing them stimulated an interest in the mystery of them that Marin himself had never felt. Yet the feeling was a familiar one, and that reminded him for the first time in many minutes: Trask, of course, would have been interested in all this. Wade Trask, physicist, electronics engineer, authority on Pripps.

Marin parked his machine and walked over to a special Taxi-Air. It had a sign up: 'Chartered.' But to those in the know, this was a private air-ferrying service to the Judge's Court. It was the only air service which was permitted to land at the Court.

The special agent in charge was dressed like a Taxi-Air driver, and the two men were well known to each other. Nevertheless, Marin had to give the password for the day and the reason for his visit. The officer gravely called Air-Control at the Court and checked the data.

Then, and not until then, they took off.

CHAPTER ELEVEN

The Taxi-Air bored deep into the misty, smoky world of industry and slum that was Pripp City.

Abruptly, a Control ship, gleaming white and with speed implied in every line, hovered above them. The radio clattered: 'Identify yourself.'

After that was done, the Taxi-Air flew on. And though other Control craft slid by above and below him, they had evidently been advised, for none questioned his right to be in this forbidden area.

Presently, in the near distance ahead, Marin saw a green parklike area. Here and there among the trees, small buildings were visible. At the far end of the park there was a cleared space. On it an arrow pointed to a sign which spelled out, in large letters, LAND HERE. Marin's driver brought his machine down on a concrete runway and rolled it to a halt under a line of trees. Marin stepped to the ground in silence. It was hard to believe that he was almost in the heart of Pripp City. A soft breeze touched his cheeks, and he could hear the vague rustling of it among the leaves. The peacefulness of the pastoral scene here on this parklike estate emphasized a certain simplicity in the Great Judge's way of life. Perhaps the simplicity was an affectation, but it always gave Marin a good feeling that it was here for him to experience – even today, when he had so many plans . . .

As he walked to the gate in the cunningly hidden fence, he saw that, as usual, the guards were uniformed Pripps. It reminded him of how much the dictator used these pariah people – openly and secretly. Perhaps, being himself a man apart, the Great Judge felt that he could ensure his own purposes only if he utilized every force of the environment. Marin did not particularly think about that, but the facsimiles of past thoughts touched the edges of his consciousness, and automatically he accepted the presence of the . . . creatures. It was said that Slater had attempted to put in his own Control men, at the time of his appointment nearly a decade earlier, but his argument had evidently not altered in any visible way the attitudes of the Great Judge.

Strange leader – to have chosen Pripps to guard him, Pripps as servants! In this case at least, the Pripp reputation for violence and treachery seemed not to apply. Service here, of course, provided individual Pripps a base for self-esteem.

The Pripp officer at the gate was rather a handsome individual in a fishy-eyed fashion. He said, 'Sir, Miss Delindy Darrell is at the private pool. She requests that you see her there for a minute, before you join the luncheon party.'

Marin nodded, not trusting himself to speak. He went on into the private grounds, and he was thinking, Things must be happening.

It would be their first meeting since . . .

He winced. And put the thought away. And wondered, Is it possible I could persuade her to come to see me somewhere?

Delindy had come out of the water and was sitting alone in the sun; she was soaking wet, and quite delightful to the eye. The glow was there, the smile, the apparent happiness at seeing him. She held out her hands, and he took them; and she looked him over with her dancing eyes, but when she spoke there was a note of anxiety in her voice. 'I want you to take me to Asia with you day after next. Will you think it over?'

Her physical reaction to her own request was startling. A mask had fallen. She was trembling. He could see the pulse of swift heartbeat in her throat, the quick rise and fall of her bosom, and the trembling of her hands. She whispered, 'Please consider it. But now, if I should be asked why you came, what shall I say?'

'The children,' Marin asked, 'how are –' he hesitated '– our children?'

'Just great,' she said, and she smiled wanly. The pulsing in her throat ceased. Her breathing grew normal. Color swarmed into her cheeks. She smiled, more warmly, impulsively. 'I'm glad you asked, dear.' She let go his hands. 'You'd better go.'

Marin said, 'I'd like very much for you to go with me.'

He walked away; and now it was he who was trembling slightly. So she wanted to go to the Jorgian border with him on the eve of war. Did she suspect that this was to be the attack?

He came to the luncheon 'room', and now his attention concentrated on the Great Judge and on the reason for the luncheon.

The lunch was to be held in a small building built –

43

according to the legend engraved in the stone supporting the roof of the veranda – of fine granite stone gathered from all over the world. No quarry had contributed more than half a dozen pieces. The building was a gift to the Great Judge from the grateful people of a country in old Europe that had been conquered some eight years before. The entire parklike area was made up of such small buildings, each a donation, each representing the ultimate in fine interiors, costly and beautiful materials, gracious architecture. In such an atmosphere, entirely without the glitter of large buildings, the Great Judge lived with his women, his current cronies, and his Pripp servants.

As Marin entered the high-ceilinged luncheon room, he saw that in one corner – at a distance from the orchestra dais – was a table set for eight. More than a dozen Pripp waiters stood in several groups near the kitchen. And, in the lounge alcove, sipping drinks, were the other guests.

He recognized them all: a playwright, a famous interpretive musician, a card player, and three other men less easy to label. They were the fabulous companion type, men with quick tongues, a gift for storytelling and the easy genius that goes with understanding great problems without the bias of concern as to outcome. For Marin, the Jorgian campaign would normally have been a matter of prestige. For these men, had they known about it, it would be table conversation.

There was an exchange of greetings. Marin accepted a drink from the playwright, parried a couple of comments about his private life, and then studied the men who had been invited by the Great Judge on this particular occasion to participate in this particular gathering.

What interested him about the luncheon was that it was not, strictly speaking, necessary. The Jorgian affair could not be discussed. Besides, short of canceling the invasion, the leader could say nothing at this late hour that could affect, or interfere with, such an immensity of small movements.

There was a stirring at the outer door.

The man who entered the room then bore very little resemblance to the ordinary conception of what a dictator was like. This was an angry man. He was so angry that no one ever thought of dealing with him on a rational level. Here was a person with whom you agreed – or you died. Marin had always agreed with him. It was a curious compromise within himself, an attitude based on what he had always believed to be a total acceptance of the other's goals. Within that framework of similar assumptions, he moved freely, made decisions, acted – without fear of doing anything that would arouse the unreasoning rage of the great man.

Ivan Prokov, better known as the Great Judge, was well built and just under six feet tall. He wore a pink silk shirt, white silk trousers and a white scarf-tie around his neck. He had a leonine head, a commanding appearance and a score of deceptive personalities. He waved now at the others and walked rapidly toward Marin with outstretched hand.

'David,' he said warmly.

He caught Marin's arm and urged him toward the luncheon table. 'You've not much time,' he said. 'So let's begin eating.'

And that was virtually all the conversation there was between the Great Judge and himself – except for the conversational atmosphere provided by the luncheon group.

Marin, who had hard work ahead of him, busied himself with his food, a delicious creation of oysters and rice and vegetables in a sauce. The others quickly became absorbed in an animated discussion on the subject, Should there be an inquiry at this early stage into the success, or lack of success, of the group laws and group practices? And, if so, who should conduct the inquiry?

Marin found himself presently wondering who had initiated the controversial argument. And he couldn't help but note that things were being said which, if they were ever produced in a courtroom, would automatically require convictions. He could not recall ever having heard so much seditious talk in the presence of the Great Judge.

Abruptly that gave him his only real clue. He was being tested. After his defense of Trask in the council, a doubt had arisen in the mind of the dictator.

Marin felt a strange thrill of anxiety. It was a new experience for him. Twice, during a lull in the conversation, he looked up to find the Great Judge watching him. The second time the man said, 'What organizations, or individuals, would you turn such an inquiry over to, David?'

It was easy to answer that, now that he suspected the test. He

45

said smoothly, 'My first choice would be Medellin and Slater.'

The great man chuckled. 'It is a choice that would not have occurred to me,' he said frankly.

Marin said, 'Would you care to have me take the matter under advisement in a week or so and report to you then?'

The Great Judge frowned. 'I might. But I really have other, more important things for you to do. So don't dwell on it.'

He became absorbed with his food, and there was a thoughtful expression on his face. But it was he who finally glanced at his watch, and said, 'Time you were on your way, David. Good luck.'

And that was the luncheon.

On his way to the military airport Marin went over what had happened, and it seemed to him finally that he had been there to be looked over. The Great Judge was unhappy about his defense of Trask, and he had wanted to savor his presence.

It was difficult to decide what the dictator had concluded; and – Marin told himself – there was really no use thinking about it. For the moment at least, the Great Judge's opinion of him was a minor problem. He had a job to do, time to waste, and time to save.

CHAPTER TWELVE

Marin arrived at Rocket Take-Off a few minutes before two. The field nestled in a valley twenty miles north of the city. Corroded, barren, a typically bleak military encampment, the valley was in its entire length uninhabited except by military personnel, and there were no buildings or structures that were not there for military use. At the extreme northern end of the area, where the land began to be hilly and rugged, a series of concrete bunkers and runways marked the take-off zone. The rocket plane itself stood in the shelter of an overhanging wing of a giant concrete bunker.

As Marin's hopjet landed, the activity around the stubby-winged rocket plane seemed to become more feverish. Seen from the air, it had looked almost sedate. As Marin walked over, he had the impression of numerous little machines darting around aimlessly, pulling empty trucks and full trucks, or pulling nothing at all. He saw also that several men were standing in a group near the steep gangplank. One of the men was a big young fellow with a boy's face. Two were granite-faced older men. Another had bleak eyes but a smiling face. It was this individual who showed Marin a badge identifying him as a plain-clothes Control officer, and it was he who indicated the big youth.

'Mr. Marin, this is the young man Mr. Slater mentioned to you.'

There were hissings and thunderings and the sound of voices and of movements of men and machines. And so the introduction was incomplete. 'Mr. Marin, I want you to meet –' wail of sound '– Burnley.'

Marin shook hands with the heavy-set young man who was bigger than he was by inches all around. He guessed that the youngster's age was twenty or less; and in that first look he seemed to bear no resemblance whatsoever to the Great Judge. There was something familiar about him, but what it was he had no time to determine. The speedy little tractors and two trucks were buzzing off. Men were going down into concrete shelters, and the field in the vicinity of the giant rocket plane began to look deserted.

The pilot paused beside Marin. 'Sir, we're ready when you are.' He moved on up into the machine.

Young Burnley got a timid look into his soft brown eyes. 'I'd better get aboard.'

He was almost impolite in his haste, for he hurried up the gangplank as if he feared he might be left behind. Marin followed more slowly, pondering what he would do with Burnley. His estimate was that the youth had no real ability for self-determined action. Such men could become craftsmen under the command of fear, but they must not command. The realization disappointed him. The Great Judge would be unhappy.

Marin settled into the seat beside the young man and dutifully strapped himself in. The pilot had evidently been waiting for him to come aboard, for the doors wheezed shut, the seats tilted noiselessly, and there was a muffled thunder of rockets and a pressure of ultra-rapid movement. The pressure continued for many minutes as the projectile climbed slant-ingly into the sky. The rockets shut off abruptly, and the machine followed its curving course at the outer edges of the Earth's atmosphere. It began to fall presently, and Marin turned to his companion. Young Burnley had his eyes closed and was lying back, looking very relaxed.

To Marin, it was still a case of fond, fatherly eyes seeing a resemblance which he himself could not detect. If this boy were the son of the Great Judge, then for the leader that identification provided the clue of recognition. Oh, Great Judge, he wondered, have you been misled? Exact records were kept, of course, on the outcome of the mating games. But no record keeper of the less-organized early days could guarantee what a woman might have been doing the night before the games.

'What's your first name?' Marin asked.

'David.'

'Well, well, my name also,' said Marin.

'That's right, sir. I was named after you.'

A staggering moment . . . Recovery.

Marin's memory raced back to the first mating games. A number of women had sent him their tokens, and though he was only seventeen years of age and ineligible by law, there were enough loopholes in those days for a man, with his mother's influence, to get to the starting line. A skillful application of make-up had brought him up to the age minimum, so far as appearance was concerned. Excitement, the egotism of youth, an enormous physical vitality, had won for him two victories in the field and the right to impregnate two women.

Marin turned in his seat, the better to look at the boy; and saw that the young man was flushing. 'Well,' he said, 'tell me about yourself.'

David Burnley, it turned out, had grown up in a small west coast community, one of three children of a woman named Ethel Burnley. 'I was the only famous child,' said David Burnley, with a note of pride in his voice. 'Mother never got near a man as great as you again, and I guess she didn't do George and Sarah any good by talking about it.'

Marin presumed that George and Sarah were the other two children, but he said nothing. He was disturbed to realize that he couldn't remember either of those first two women by whom he had had children.

Young Burnley continued. 'Mother worked in one of the public nurseries, and so I saw a lot of her and didn't have the same feeling of being lost that some of the other children had. Of course, they got over that but—'

'What schooling have you had?' Marin asked.

'I'm in the middle of college. This is vacation where we are. It'll be over at the end of September. I'm majoring in political economics.'

It appeared that he had not expected such an assignment as this 'with my own father', though he had put in for government service during his vacation. 'Of course, I listed your name, and maybe that's what did it – but it was a surprise just the same.'

It was obvious that it had been done deliberately by someone; and it reminded Marin that, despite all the effort to minimize the role of the father, people still thought in terms of bringing a father and his son together and did not seriously abide by the rule which said that this was nepotism, and that any return to the old-fashioned marriage system would tend to enslave women once more.

A woman was paid a government allowance for the support of her children. The entire male population, whether they won at the games or not, or even whether they qualified or not, paid the taxes from which the allowance derived.

While the mother must look after the children, and provide them with personal care, public nurseries took them off her hands for a specified maximum of hours a week, which she and the children could agree upon. While no woman had to put her children in the nurseries the maximum permissible time, a minimum allotment was mandatory. By law, a woman could not be caught up completely in the role of motherhood.

The method had certain good ideas in it. There was no doubt that a sharp look had been taken at the history of woman, and an attempt made to free her.

Sitting there, Marin recalled a survey made by the Group Masters Council. Thirty-eight per cent of the adult male and female population had sought a private alleviation which included scores of methods for a man and a woman and her children to maintain a family relationship. Men became boarders in such homes, or lived next door, or across the street.

Beside Marin, the youth said, 'This is sure a fast flight. How long does it take?'

Marin didn't have time to answer. The ship had been curving downward on a long slant for some time. Now, abruptly, their seats swung fully around. A moment later the forward rockets roared up and began to apply braking power.

Conversation was instantly impossible. Marin sat with eyes closed and urgently regretted that this father–son relationship had come up to disturb his activity in the most important week of his life. His past was spotted with interest he had taken from time to time in his children. On one occasion, when he had been motivated to investigate what manner of offspring he had achieved, that three year-old who was the subject of his interest had shrieked with rage during his entire visit.

Actually, the response was sensationally significant, suggesting an awareness of who he was on a feeling level of life.

CHAPTER THIRTEEN

They came down in the darkness of early, early morning. Here, at the edge of Siberia, it was not yet dawn, and all that was visible below was a vast spread of colored lights. Amid those lights an army was encamped. It was one of many such which ringed the entire mountain state of Jorgia. This was Camp A, and it actually dated from the end of the Third Atomic War. Gradually, over the years, the number of men and machines had been increased until – for three years now – it had been a formidable army.

During a score of years, which included some of the most frigid winters on record, the 'city' that was Camp A had acquired many permanent characteristics, most of which could not be seen in the darkness. But Marin knew that there were concrete runways, plane hangars and several vast airfields, and – what was even more costly in such a remote area – a Rocket Take-Off and Landing.

The big plane came throbbing down out of the darkness,

rockets still reversed. Since magnetic equipment was useless for large machines, and since no one had ever figured out how such a stubby-winged monster could come in slowly, the pilot and the ground radar co-operated in the intricate process of a 500-mile-an-hour landing. Just before contact the lowered wheels were spun at terrific speed, so that the tearing effect on the tires was minimized. For a long, long time – so it seemed – the machine floated along with the rubber barely touching the concrete, the rockets spitting fire, a fine balance maintained by automatic machinery.

Eventually that perfect co-ordination of electronic equipment slowed the machine to the point where efficient manual control was possible. The plane swung off the main runway and, coasting still, rolled with tugging brakes to a brilliantly lighted concrete overhang. It came to a full stop so gently that a moment passed before Marin could untense himself and realize that the great violence of movement had ceased.

Beside him, young Burnley said, 'Gosh!'

The outer doors wheezed open. Marin led the way down the gangplank, and presently he was introducing the youth to a group of officers and civilian representatives of his department. It was, he discovered, 4.20 A.M. at Camp A, and he guessed that a lot of sleepy people had gotten up for him.

Waiting cars drove the entire party to an official residence, which was large enough to have an auditorium in it. Marin took his son into the library and suggested to the boy that he begin familiarizing himself with the political and economic problems of Jorgia. 'I'd particularly like,' he said, 'for you during the next few days to examine the current leadership structure of the state and get data for me on names and positions and relative importance of various individuals and jobs.'

Young Burnley was brisk. 'I'll do what I can, sir. I already have a background in the field.'

Marin left the library and checked with the technicians who would handle the multiple electronic devices and monitor the meters attached to each chair in the auditorium. The electronics department had two jobs to do. There would be people present who would not understand the English language. Translation would be supplied through earphones from translating machines. The translation principle used was the same as that in automatic phones and automatic typing machines, where plastic models of the electrical impulses of sound activated the essential mechanisms. The second task of the electronic machines was to identify spies. Marin satisfied himself that the technicians in charge were qualified to evaluate the data which the needles would register from each individual chair.

Marin had coffee with the technicians and a group of officers, and the details of the meeting were gone into again. He learned that most of the Jorgia agents were already in camp and that the plan was to return them to Jorgia by plane and let each individual seek his own home territory from selected landing points. It was believed that some of them would be picked up, but it was considered doubtful that the information gained from one or several individuals would actually reach the proper authorities in time for counteraction to be taken.

Marin made no direct comment on their presumption. But he did not doubt that a spy system existed. He'd better warn his son not to speak to strangers.

A liaison officer entered. 'Sir, the people are beginning to assemble in the auditorium.'

Marin stood by. 'I'd better get dressed,' he said. 'Call me when the assembly is complete.'

He went to his apartment, changed his clothes, and then headed for the library. Because of his purpose, he entered by way of a stairway from a basement which was a repository of old files. The entrance itself was a little hallway with drapes closing it off from the library proper.

Marin paused behind the drapes and heard his son say, 'What will happen then?'

'Nothing.' It was a man's baritone voice. 'All we want to do is get him into a drugged, hypnotic state, and then we'll indoctrinate him against war. We've got to start somewhere, and there's no time to lose. Listen: after the meeting we'll get him in here through you. We'll have you tied up, so he won't suspect anything . . .'

Marin ever so gently parted the drapes. A tall, dark-haired man of about thirty was bending over David, who sat behind a desk. The youth's face was white and tense. Half a dozen feet away stood a short, stocky man. He held a blaster, and he was looking toward the door that led to the main hallway, on the opposite side of which was the rear entrance to the auditorium, where the meeting was to be held. The stocky man was as nervous as the tall man was apparently relaxed.

No one else was visible.

With narrowed eyes, Marin drew out his blaster. He felt no mercy. The two men had selected their weapon by having a destroying energy instrument instead of the less lethal gas guns. So be it.

In a single, co-ordinated movement, Marin sent a full blast of energy at the man with the weapon. As he saw him go down, his head a blackened mass, he stepped through the drapes – and fired at the tall individual. His clothes smoking, the man spun over and fell in a limp heap on the floor.

Marin walked out into the room and said grimly, 'All right, David, let's have the whole story. You—' He stopped. The young man had been watching him, his lower jaw sagging slightly but his eyes alert, his manner one of bright awareness.

The look of him changed. The brightness faded. The awareness went out of him. He leaned forward on the desk, almost as if a great weariness had come upon him, and he sprawled there limply.

Fainted! Marin thought in abrupt contempt.

But it shook him more than the traitorism. Cowardice, weakness – his son! The shame of it burned deep.

He walked over, grabbed the slickly combed hair, and, lifting the head, slapped the boy's face resoundingly; and already the thought was on him: I've got to hurry! I've got to get the whole story from him before the meeting and decide what to do with him.

In his urgent anger, he slapped the flabby face a dozen times. And then something about the feel of the skin brought a perception from his own vast experience with men in all stages of unconsciousness. It was a death feel. Startled, he released his hold, reached for the big youth's hand, and took his pulse. Nothing.

Marin pushed the body back in the chair and, bending down, listened for a heartbeat. Slowly he straightened. He was shocked and incredulous – and something else. It was not grief, he told himself. It was not even a sentimental notion that he *ought* to feel grief for a youngster he hadn't known until a few hours before. But he knew what it was. One of his life lines had been broken off.

Children were a projection into the future. A tragedy of the Great Judge's group world was that nearly 70 per cent of men, having failed at the mating games, were forbidden by law to carry forward the life stream that flowed through them, beyond them, from prehistoric times. For them, it was the end of the line. The great randomness of gene variation was being deliberately cut.

The shock ran its course. He began to think again. And to act. He stepped to the phone and called the office of the residence. When a man's voice answered, he said, 'This is David Marin. Send a doctor to the library. Get an ambulance and have a guard unit come in at once.'

He hung up. And, for a moment, he was not disturbed. Men had died before in his presence, principally from torture, sometimes from an overdose of gas or drug. And they had been brought back to life by doctors, trained in the special resuscitation methods of the Control.

He knelt beside the tall man and searched him. He found a key ring, a small notebook and a pen, a billfold containing money but nothing else, and a comb and handkerchief.

Marin slipped the notebook into his pocket; he was about to bend down and search the stocky man when the door opened. Marin straightened warily, gas gun ready. But it was the guard unit that came in – six soldiers and an officer.

The officer took the scene in, apparently at a glance, and motioned his men. 'Guard the windows and doors!' he said. He faced Marin. 'Doctor is on his way from next door. What's happened, sir?'

Marin ignored the question. He wasn't sure yet what he wanted to have had happen, public-wise. He said, 'This boy is dead, seemingly only from shock. Nothing actually happened to him, so far as I know. I want the doctor to use every possible facility to bring him back to life. And remove these bodies.'

'Very good, sir.'

Marin hesitated. It was time to leave, time to be at the meeting. Yet he didn't want to go. If they brought David Burnley back to life, he wanted to be present. The boy might say things that would arouse suspicion.

Over at the desk young Burnley stirred. Marin didn't think of it as a life movement but as an unbalancing of a dead weight. He jumped to catch the body before it could fall to the floor. As he grasped the youth's arm, he felt the muscles tugging under the skin. Then swiftness of the reintegration that followed nullified any advance thought about it.

David Burnley sat up, looked blank for a moment, and then said in a frightened tone, 'What was that thing in my mind?'

Unexpected remark. Marin drew back. 'Thing!' he said.

'Something came into my mind and took control. I could feel it. I—' He stopped. Tears came into his eyes.

The officer strode over. 'Anything I can do?'

Marin waved him away. 'Get that doctor!' he said.

It was a defensive action. He needed time here to grasp a new idea. He was remembering what Slater had said, about the use of electronic circuits directly into the brains of human beings as a method of control from a distance . . . That boy was dead, Marin thought tensely.

Dead without visible cause. Was it possible that, as the 'circuit' connection was broken, or even dissolved, death resulted?

Again, he had no time to think about it clearly. It seemed to mean that young Burnley was a victim, not a traitor. It seemed to mean that the 'death' might have broken the connection, though that was not certain.

Marin said gently, 'How do you feel, David?'

'Why, all right, sir.' He stood up, swayed, and then righted himself, smiling warmly. He braced himself visibly. 'All right,' he said again.

Marin said, 'I'll have someone help you to a bed. And David—'

'Yes?'

'Say nothing to anyone until I have a chance to talk to you later.'

He spoke in a tone of command; and, without waiting for a response, called over two of the guardsmen and watched them half carry, half lead the young man out of the room. Then, tautly conscious that his main job remained to be done, Marin returned to his own apartment. He was slightly surprised to discover that the call to attend the meeting had not yet come. Restlessly, he waited.

The more he thought about what had happened, the more disturbed he became. 'Some *thing* came into my mind and took control!' young Burnley had said. If that were true, then it was an event of such importance that perhaps nothing else could compare to it.

It would have had to be preplanned. Marin was very sure of that. The circuit that made it possible for something to take control would have had to be installed at some earlier time.

Marin sighed, opened the transparent plastic doors, and went out into the garden. Dawn was breaking, though the sun had not yet come up. The air was fresh, even brisk. It was difficult to realize that, a short time before, he had been in the Judge's City, and that it was still mid-afternoon in that distant capital.

Standing there in the gray light, he recalled that he was in the land that had cradled the first important Authoritarian group movement. Here, in the heartland of a planet, two centuries before, the Soviet Union had been born, and – before even proving their value – had spread its doctrines by force.

Blood spurted into the soil of many a land, as the ignorant and sophisticated alike sought to grapple with an idea that, on promises alone, swept aside the anchor points of history. In many countries, men, awakened by Western civilization from the apathy of the centuries, were caught up by unscrupulous and equally ignorant demagogues and were lost before they ever had a single free thought of their own. And, just as the sullen child manifests hatred of its father by bullying the neighborhood toddlers, so an exploited people, it was found, could easily be led to hate anyone except the true culprit. And so to the mental reversals and insanities of open rage, the need to strike dead, the inner movements and the outer actions of physical violence.

There were altogether three major atomic wars. At last a decimated human race emerged from the deep bunkers, and most of them, in their great weariness, did not resist as a new leader said, 'We will join the group *and* the free-enterprise idea. These are thoughts and desires which seem to spring from the heart. One binds the body to a warm interrelationship with other bodies; the other frees the spirit. One gives life to the individual through his community; the other recognizes his right to be individually creative.'

And then the Great Judge had added, 'In the confusion of war's end, many areas will be long without adequate government. Temporary states will form there, and will rigidify, and will seek to perpetuate themselves. We warn these people now. The history of the last two centuries does not permit us to be merciful. We will tolerate no separations.'

Nearly a thousand separate states formed, most of them small and insignificant, and many of them primitive in their politics and in their economy. In some cases, a few individuals elevated themselves to the greatness of absolute power; and from that height looked fearfully around and wondered how long it would last. It was then that the whispering began, the diplomatic maneuvering, the continual soothing statements from a thousand sources, that the Great Judge had been hasty in his early remarks, that he did not mean them to be taken literally, and that indeed he had spoken out of the tension of the moment. Just how many of the soothings originated with the Great Judge no one would ever clearly know. But in twenty years the original thousand states had become a hundred.

The fall of Jorgia would probably bring another twenty-five or so hurrying to make agreements, which – whatever the wording – would mean their eventual incorporation into a single world state.

Footsteps sounded behind Marin. It was an official to tell him that all was in readiness.

CHAPTER FOURTEEN

There were about a hundred men and women. Each individual, Marin had been informed, claimed to represent from twenty to fifty units, or groups. Which meant that a total of some ten thousand people had their ears in this room, by way of delegates. There would be a spy or two of the Jorgian Queen's among them. Whoever it was would be caught within the hour and dealt with before Marin's departure.

Marin came out in a private's uniform. It was neatly pressed, and actually very skillfully tailored to set him off to advantage. But it was designed to influence people who regarded themselves as idealists and who desperately wanted their small state to become a part of the politico-economic system of the Great Judge.

Jorgia was, in actuality, a political monstrosity. A group of West European adventurers had taken it over after the collapse of the world's armed forces, and they had done a whole series of strange things. First, they had set up a scientific military state. This rapidly evolved into some thirty segment states, each under the control of a corporation. There was a period of confusion, from which the original leader of the adventurers had emerged as hereditary king – a fantastic assumption of powers and dignities which nevertheless seemed to be acceptable to the conservative elements. Early democratic procedures were suspended after the assassination of the 'king'. Under the rule of the eldest daughter, an entirely hierarchical system rigidified itself and prepared to defend itself against the Great Judge. It was not surprising that many Jorgians resented the loss of right and so became willing agents of the Great Judge.

And here they were.

Marin raised his hands for silence, and said, 'Men and women of Jorgia, I am informed that you have determined in your councils that approximately a thousand present leaders of the Jorgian regime must be assassinated, or executed, if captured. I must inform you that no advance action is to be taken against the Queen.'

He placed no other restraint on them. Actually, because of the pain-inducing circuit which could be impressed on each person's muscles, death in most cases would not be necessary. But these men and women knew nothing of that remarkable control device.

He went on: 'Whomever you feel it necessary to kill, be sure that you plan the assassination carefully. In the early hours of a revolution certain leaders can rally so much support to themselves that they imperil the entire operation.'

He felt no particular mercy for the men involved. Knowing what he did of the countless millions who had lost their lives in the three atomic wars, he felt impatience with men who had once more tried to set up a separate state, with all that that meant in terms of future war potential.

The audience seemed impressed by his earnestness. They sat

in silence as Marin began his detailed account of what must be accomplished. He finished that portion of his instructions with the statement: 'Each of you will be given a list of what must be done. Commit this list to memory, since it will be written in ink that will fade suddenly.'

That was a misleading statement. The instructions were not written in ink. They were impressed electronically on a special substance that looked like paper. The electronic pattern on each sheet would be destroyed by remote control, and another pattern in the 'paper' would be activated briefly and then nullified. Any subsequent attempt to reproduce the patterns would bring out a confusion of meaningless forms. The method was a development of Trask Electronics.

The moment had come for the statements of reward. One by one, Marin listed them; and now he was alert to reactions. It was at such times as this, particularly, that people gave themselves away. If there were a spy of the Jorgian Queen's among the throng of rebels, he would squirm with inner rage as he heard his country's top positions and treasures bartered away. The lie detectors, cunningly attached to each chair, would tell a part of the story. But, over and above the detective power of the sensitive instruments, Marin trusted his own acute ability to read the meaning of conflict in a man's face and in the movements of his body.

At the very beginning he had picked out a tall man of about thirty, intellectual looking, sitting stiffly about half-way to the rear. Presently, satisfied that he had his man, Marin gave the prearranged signal, and a moment later was handed a slip of paper which stated, 'Instruments verify your discovery.'

Even as he read the note he saw from the corners of his eyes that Control officers were coming along the aisles. As they came opposite their victim, they turned as of one accord, bustled past other seated individuals, and swiftly surrounded the man.

The spy grew rigid. And then, evidently recognizing the completeness of his capture, made not a single defensive move. The Control men brought him in on the stage.

Marin quieted the audience. 'This arrest was made for your protection. We have reason to believe that this man is a spy. Perhaps some one among you may recognize him when his disguise is removed.'

The entire affair must have had an unreal quality for the victim. At this hour, when it was too late, he began to struggle. He was carried to a chair and held there while a chemist came in wheeling a carriage with many trays on it. The laboratory man was in no hurry, but he did his job. He tested the hair, the eyebrows, the cheeks, the ears and the jaws and mouth. He used one chemical after another; and he did not miss.

The prisoner changed before the eyes of the audience. His sandy blond hair became dark brown. His face grew thin and sallow. His eyes lost their steely blue look and showed a terrified brown.

Suddenly a woman in the audience shouted, 'It's Kuda!'

Marin looked questioningly off stage where one of his subordinates was hastily writing a message on a blackboard. The message read: 'Jorgian society – high political family.'

Marin walked to the front of the stage. 'Ladies and gentlemen, I am sure you will agree that we are capable of handling Kuda – and any of his society friends – and I am sure you are aware that for you there are more important things than dealing with a spy. Go about your lawful business. We'll see one another in three days – at Itnamu. In the name of the Great Judge, I salute you, the future leaders of the province of Jorgia.'

They cheered him, a little hysterically, shakily. Some of them would be dead within three days, a possibility which they very likely did not dwell upon; and certainly he had no intention of telling them that statistics of past revolutions indicated an average of 20 per cent casualties among the leadership.

As they began to stream out, Marin turned to the guards holding the spy. 'Search him thoroughly; then bring him to the library. I'll take care of him.'

As Marin entered the library a minute later, he saw that his son, David Burnley, was sitting behind the desk where, earlier, he had 'died'. Frowning, Marin walked toward the young man, who stood up and came to attention. 'Why aren't you in bed, David?'

'This is my duty.' There was a high color in the youth's face. 'I felt all right, and I insisted . . . and they could find nothing wrong with me.' He broke off. 'I've been getting together the material you wanted.' He looked anxious to please.

Momentarily Marin was undecided. What had happened to

his son was actually more important for his own purposes than the Jorgian spy. And so, one minute – two minutes now – was worth a lot indeed.

He said, 'David, that thing in your mind – how long was it there?'

'When the men came in I felt it.'

'You knew them?'

'I never saw them before. But they knew me.'

Marin did a rapid mental check. Slater . . . the Great Judge . . . some Control deputies, personnel of the government service in charge of assignment – enough, he thought, who knew of this trip, enough for a leak to have occurred.

David Burnley was speaking. 'They had heard I had ideals, that I was against war. I talked too much, I guess, at college. They asked if I would co-operate with them. I started to say no. I swear that, sir. And then this feeling came into my mind. And something seized my tongue, and I heard myself say, "Yes". They immediately explained that they wanted to get control of you, so you wouldn't fight this war. And I kept agreeing against my will.' He was trembling as he made his confession. 'I swear, sir—'

Marin said, 'Never mind. I believe you.'

He did. The 'death' had been too real, and the first words spoken when the boy regained consciousness had been convincingly involuntary. The plan of the two spies had not been too bad, really. And what an achievement it would have been if they had reached to the commander-in-chief on the eve of battle and controlled him by hypnotic drugs.

Someone knocked at the door. Marin came out of his introspection and went to the door. It was the guard with Kuda. 'One moment!' he said, and closed the door. He returned to his son. 'We want to question a spy in here. Will you take your papers and books and go out in the garden?'

David Burnley started to gather his material and then he paused. 'Could I stay and listen?' he asked.

Marin said no. 'We haven't time for a long questioning, so we're going to get rough.'

The youth lost some of his high color. He took up his books and started toward the door. There he slowed and turned. 'Is force absolutely necessary?'

'No,' said Marin. 'Force is never necessary.'

'But then, why—' The big young man looked bewildered.

'If the prisoner,' said Marin steadily, 'will tell us what we want to know, no one will lay a hand upon him.' He smiled sardonically at the boy, who was biting his lip. It was evident that young Burnley was guessing that the spy might be recalcitrant.

'In addition,' said Marin, 'we may want to change his mind about certain things and send him back to Jorgia as our agent. We doubt that he will do this unless we use certain persuasive methods.'

The youth was trembling visibly. 'But you can't expect him to become your agent. Why, people just don't do things like that.'

Marin said in his most matter-of-fact manner, 'The great problem is our time shortage. We don't lack for methods.' He broke off. 'I'll see you later.'

Young Burnley paused at the door in a final demonstration of his reluctance to leave. 'What are these methods you use?'

'First of all,' said Marin, 'we issue the greatest shock of all. We go through the formality of sentencing him to death.'

CHAPTER FIFTEEN

For a while after the forcible indoctrination, the condemned man raved. It was difficult for Marin, watching from the other side of the room, to grasp any continuity in the words. But the sounds were angry, the manner violent.

The fury subsided suddenly. The tall, hollow-eyed prisoner muttered something under his breath and then sank into a chair. He sat there tensely; the very way his clothes hung on him projected the rigidity of the muscles underneath. His brown eyes had the dazed appearance of ultimate shock. They looked hopeless. They pleaded. They seemed irrational with fear and grief.

The silence ended in a drama of slow motion. The victim climbed slowly to his feet and, with dragging feet, began to pace back and forth before the great window, where the dawn light was brighter now. At irregular intervals the man mumbled something; again, Marin could only make out an occasional word. No meaning came through.

He watched the spectacle with narrowed eyes. He was aware of his companion – a Control agent, evidently not too accustomed to violence – leaning toward him. 'Who'd have thought a man like him would go to pieces?'

Marin said, 'I've seen people break down before.' He felt stiff but determined. 'After you've seen it a few times you know roughly what can be done.'

He paused, in spite of himself, remembering. For a moment the black shadows of his past flickered in his eyes. No particular picture came into his mind, but a conglomerate of grim impressions, a flicker of faces that stared and twitched and sagged, having only one thing in common: in all of them were written fear, grief, hopelessness and pain.

His companion ventured, finally: 'What are you waiting for, sir? After all, he seems amenable.'

Marin did not reply but instead stood up abruptly, and walked across the room, making as if to pass the unsteady spy. As the latter staggered unseeingly toward him, Marin stepped deliberately into his path, and while pretending to avoid him, actually gave him a shove. Kuda fell awkwardly to the floor, onto his knees. He crouched there, cringing oddly, like a whipped dog; then he stumbled to his feet. He continued his unsteady pacing, the collision already apparently forgotten.

Marin walked through into the adjoining room, to give face to the appearance of accident of what had happened.

He took out the notebook, which he had removed from one of the dead men earlier. There were several entries: a few phone numbers, what seemed to be an expense account, several pages of initials in series of two- or three-name initials, Marin guessed, and five written notations. One of these read:

W. T. death sentence	8/26
Attack on J. sched	8/30
Destroy evidence	8/29
Destroy records	8/30//31//9/1
Destroy equip.	9/1/2
All cell leaders leave J.	9/1//2//3—not later

Marin studied the message, shocked and incredulous. 'W.T. death sentence – *Wade Trask*.' August 26 was the date the sentence had been handed down. The attack on J. (Jorgia) *was* scheduled for the thirtieth, but that latter date was known only to the Great Judge, Slater, Medellin and himself. All the Group Masters knew that the attack was to be made, but they didn't know the date.

Marin's gaze flashed down to the phrase *cell leaders*. That was a Communist term, not used for a quarter of a century – certainly not used by the Jorgian government.

He returned the notebook to his pocket and called his electronics staff to bring a lie detector.

Presently they had the instruments arranged, and Kuda sitting in a chair, staring doggedly at the floor. He answered all the questions, a faraway note in his voice.

His name? Josephus Kuda. Parentage? Youngest son of Georgi Kuda, Jorgian minister of agriculture.

The story, as it came out, was simple: The Jorgian government did not know if this war scare was any more urgent than in past years. As one of the government spies among the rebel group, Kuda had the usual instructions to discover what he could. He did not regard this calling together of the rebel delegates as decisive, because similar scary actions had been taken before. He knew nothing of the two men Marin had killed.

Marin said, almost blankly, 'But, then, who are they?'

He had the dead bodies brought in. Kuda stared at them dully and shook his head. The lie detector verified his negation.

The Control officer said, 'Shall we indoctrinate him and send him back to Jorgia as our agent?'

Marin shook his head. He did not say it, but the fact was it would serve no useful purpose, with the attack only two days away.

The man said, 'What disposition shall be made?'

'One moment,' said Marin.

He walked to the garden door and called his son. David Burnley came bustling in; he was like an overgrown boy, in a wide-eyed, gawking, awkward fashion. He stared at the prisoner; and Marin saw the shock of the man's condition penetrate. Instantly the boy's eyes and face became mirrors of his inner criticism.

Marin said quickly, 'We used hypnosis on him and he fell apart from terror. He'll recover.'

He paused at that point, aware that there was a defensive note in his voice. He bit his lip, wondering if perhaps he weren't falling apart also. He was definitely letting himself be influenced by the youth's opinions. He said, with greater suavity, 'Young man, I'm going to turn this prisoner over to you. I'd like you to obtain from him the names and present location of every close relative of Queen Kijshnashenia's. Our plan is to save their lives. I make this statement in the full confidence that you, as my son, will believe that I am sincere. If he provides us with that information, his family will also be spared.'

'What about him?'

'I cannot make him such an offer,' said Marin gravely. 'We do not bargain for the lives of spies. The decision to execute has been rendered. A court will have to hear any appeal for mercy.'

'Oh!'

The youth stood very still, his oversized body quivering. Then: 'Where will I keep him?'

Marin turned to the Control official. 'Keep the prisoner Kuda available for activity within the area of this residence at David Burnley's direction.'

He shook the boy's hand. 'I'll be back in two days,' he said.

'Are you leaving right away?'

'No, but I won't see you again before I depart.'

The feeling of time pressure was returning. He had forced himself to relax in the face of the inevitable. But now the Jorgian interlude for this day was almost at an end. Another hour's discussion with staff officers, just to make sure that certain eventualities had been taken into account; and then . . .

CHAPTER SIXTEEN

It was a few minutes after nine when the rocket plane came whistling down out of the upper atmosphere. It floated for miles on the Valley Rocket Landing near the Judge's City and finally slowed down to manually controllable speeds. It wheeled with easy power over to the Discharge gate. And Marin, who had snatched a half hour of sleep en route, climbed down, ready to spend what remained of the evening on his private affairs.

He paused in mid-stride as he saw that Edmund Slater was waiting for him. In a single jump of the mind, Marin felt himself tumble back from his great position as head of an army into a pit of tension. He walked over to the Control chief. As they shook hands, Marin thought, He must be here for a reason.

Slater greeted him. 'The boss wants you to spend the night at the Court and have breakfast with him.'

Marin said, 'It will be a pleasure to have breakfast with such distinguished company. However . . .'

He couldn't believe that Slater had met him in order to deliver so minor a message. A note, a phone call, a messenger boy, would have served equally well. He had been stiffening as he spoke and as he thought. Now he felt determined not to permit anyone, neither the Great Judge nor Slater, to snatch this evening from him.

He parted his lips to say that he would go to the Court later. And then he closed them again. Because – What was on the mind of this grim little fellow? It seemed to Marin he'd better not say too much until that was clarified. Despite his outward mildness, here was a man who dealt in death and destruction.

What he did say was: 'I'm puzzled as to why you turned up to meet me, Ed.'

Slater frowned and stared at the ground. Abruptly, and visibly, he came to a decision. He looked up. 'David, I think you and I ought to go to see the Great Judge right now.'

'About what?'

'The Trask matter.'

That was staggering. Literally, he hadn't thought of anyone who was important really being concerned about Trask now. The sentence had been delivered. So far as they knew, the execution would be carried out at the appointed hour.

Marin cursed under his breath. He should have known that the human bloodhound, Slater, and the tiger of a man who dominated the planet, the Great Judge, would somehow sense that something was wrong. He had observed the faculty in the

Great Judge before. An astonishing ability to select a decisive factor out of innumerable related and unrelated data. And now he had unerringly spotted Trask as a dangerous individual.

The feeling of shock passed as swiftly as it had come. It struck Marin that this tense little man was actually doing him a favor in his own irritating way.

Marin said, 'Thanks, Ed. Of course I'll go – on your say-so. My plane or yours?'

'Mine.'

'Then I'll arrange to have mine sent over.'

Slater was impatient. 'We can do that from the air. Come along.'

Standing there, he thought for the second time on this second day after Trask's sentence, Suppose I can't become myself again – in time?

He could almost see the five days of grace that remained for Trask flashing by, gone before he could do more than struggle weakly to free himself from the trap of physical identity that had been forced upon him. In the final issue, his skill at disguise would be worthless. The pain-inducing signal by which the Control dominated the human race would unerringly strike past the outward appearance and, by sustained anguish, force him to report for . . . death.

Slater was speaking. 'David, if I tell his excellency he ought to hear you on Trask, I believe he will consent to do so, without prejudice.'

Marin's heart leaped and then sank painfully. He foresaw with sharp awareness that he could have an ultimate decision by midnight. He could not ask for a better man than Slater to intercede for Trask. Not even Medellin would be as valuable for such a purpose. And yet . . .

It was too soon. He was unready for a crisis. He hadn't yet had a chance to see if the body in the secret laboratory of Trask's apartment had regained consciousness. Until that happened, he could have no clear path to safety.

It could be, of course, that the Great Judge would accept his plea and reverse the sentence of execution. But that had little reality for Marin.

He saw that Slater was shaking his head. 'I don't know why you're hesitating, my friend. In my opinion, you may be removed from your post at any moment. Therefore, any other business you have in mind is meaningless.'

Marin said, amazed, 'Removed from my position – whatever for?'

Slater was grave. 'He's unhappy, David. He heard of your appeal on Trask's behalf, and it shocked him.'

Marin followed silently as Slater led the way to his personal hopjet.

They arrived presently at the outer perimeter of the Court's air defense. Control planes guided them in, each echelon taking over while the previous one pursued its ceaseless patrol duties. The final ship landed with them, and, before they could proceed to the gate, they were identified by the Control ship's crew and escorted to where Pripp officers took over. Inside the protected grounds, Slater turned to Marin and said, 'I suggest you let me go ahead, and you just stroll along. Join us in ten minutes.'

It was not the time to seek out Delindy, so Marin remained at the edge of the lighted fairyland of gardens.

At the end of the stated time he arrived before the modest residence of the Great Judge, an eight-room, ranch-style building connected in the rear to a building which housed several servants.

Two men sat in the shadows under a tree in the patio. Both stood up as Marin approached; but only Slater came out to the light to meet him. The little man seemed to slip out of the darkness with a gliding movement. He paused abruptly in front of Marin and said, 'David, his excellency has agreed to discuss the matter of Wade Trask.'

There was a tiny note of pride in the Control chief's voice. And it was evident that he felt he had achieved a very special success. Marin held himself outwardly calm, but a flame began to burn along his blood stream. As he walked forward, he sensed again the enormous latent anger of the man who sat waiting for him. Instinctively Marin braced himself. He was determined to make a fight of it.

And for a while, then, only the sound of his voice competed with the softer sound of the night wind. He began by presenting the same argument he had given the Group Masters Council, after they had rejected his personal request. And then he went on to describe some of Trask's inventions, and the use he had made of them. He finished finally with a personal request: 'Sir, I have come to depend on this man's genius for much of the creative work of which we are constantly in need in the forces. He has given unstintingly, withholding nothing. My feeling is that this entire matter should have been dealt with on a person-to-person basis. I believe if I had not been away when the matter was first brought up, I could have talked to him and quickly discovered what was actually on his mind when he spoke the criticism of our group system. To conclude, your excellency, I do not think this man should be executed. I believe he should be freed, and as quickly as possible.'

It was said. The plea, for whatever it was worth, was over forever. Looking back on it in a lightning glance, Marin could think of nothing else of value that he could have added. Perhaps there had been a little too much emotion in his voice, and that was bad. But the feeling had crept in. And, since this would be taken to indicate his previously known interest in the welfare of Trask, even that should not of itself influence the decision.

He waited.

There was silence there under the leaf-laden tree. It was a silence that grew prolonged as the man who sat in its shadows seemed to consider what Marin had said. A thin wind soughed through the branches; the perfume of flowers and green growth grew momentarily heavier. And then diminished as the wind died.

The leader was shaking his head. 'David,' he said, 'by this time you must know that I value you as a person and as a man with genius for military matters. Your support of Trask gave me a shock, and I have wondered for some time now what your relationship with this man is.'

'There is no relationship, sir,' said Marin, 'other than a perfectly natural one arising out of my departmental work.'

'I believe that,' said the Great Judge. 'And so I expect you to withdraw your support from him. From this moment, devote your energies to winning the Jorgian war.'

It was a direct order. Marin paled, then said, 'Consider it done.' And he smiled a strained smile.

The dictator seemed to hesitate. 'There's more to this Trask matter, David, than appears on the surface. I regret that I cannot take even you into my confidence. Please believe me, however, when I say that it is of utmost importance that Jorgia is captured rapidly.'

He paused; then: 'You might say, if the death of Trask is so vital, why not suspend the usual legal delay? I can only say, there are reasons.'

Marin thought of the notebook he had taken from a dead man. He had thought that, somehow, he could decide at such a key moment as this to show it to the Great Judge. But he couldn't do it. There were too many doubts in his own mind about the Brain . . . and the Great Judge.

In the shadows, the Great Judge stood up. 'That's all. I suggest you go to your usual guest cabin, and I'll see you at breakfast.'

For Marin, a door had closed with utter finality.

CHAPTER SEVENTEEN

Marin, a reluctant guest, walked to his 'usual' cabin. The night was cooler now and, except for the lighted pathways, much darker. Already unhappy with his situation, he entered the guesthouse. He had no feeling of needing sleep. He did have a strong conviction that he must not wholly waste this night.

And yet, by dictator's command, he would have to remain within these guarded grounds. To leave for any reason would arouse suspicion.

He undressed indecisively and took a pair of guest pajamas from a drawer but did not put them on. It semed to him that, if he got into them, it would be like a decision to go to sleep. Sleep now equaled death five days hence. It was an unpleasant mathematics, and actually there was nothing that he could add or subtract with certainty. His unwillingness to spend this second night sleeping was a feeling, not a calculation.

Naked, Marin crawled into the bed, turned out the light, and lay in the darkness. He couldn't help but remember his now-overdue appointment with Ralph Scudder, the Pripp leader. Not that he had any plan for using Scudder, but his failure to meet the other had the look of a lost opportunity.

Marin reached over and set the alarm dial of the illuminated bed clock. *Sleep*, he thought gloomily. At least he'd be rested for tomorrow.

He awoke with a start, conscious that someone else was in the room.

A woman whispered in the dark, 'David!'

Delindy!

Marin whispered back, 'Come over here to the bed.'

There was a pause, a movement, the scent of perfume; and then a tug on the sheets, and she was in the bed beside him. She pressed up to him, and he became aware that she had on a silken negligee. It felt cool against his skin.

'You wretch,' she chided. 'No clothes on.'

But her fingers moved, gently, restlessly, over his body, as she said, 'I can't stay. How will I meet you, and go with you?'

Marin kissed her. Her lips were soft and responsive, but he could feel the tension in her body. He said, 'Dress your hair simply, and don't wear any make-up. I'll notify Air Command a lady is going along.'

There was silence in the darkness beside him. Marin said finally, 'How does that strike you?'

'Not very flattering,' said the woman.

Marin said softly, 'Now, dear, you know it's not make-up that creates the beautiful Delindy, and I know it. But let's not get tangled up in unnecessary disguises. How are you explaining your absence to the Great Judge?'

'Oh, I'm just going away for a day or so. He doesn't mind.'

'Have you told him where you're going?'

'No. He doesn't require explanations.'

In the darkness, Marin shook his head ever so slightly. She had been taken in by the outward appearance of complete tolerance. The inward reality, Marin was convinced, was not the tendency to suspicion that had disturbed so many observers. It was simply, and straightforwardly, an incredible astuteness of perception combined with the very rage which the man detested. The Great Judge was a nonpareil genius who looked into the hearts of men, and when he saw there the rage he unconsciously divined in himself, he struck dead the offending insanity before it could shake his own inner stability.

Marin said gently, 'Let me instruct you exactly what you do. Do you mind?'

'I'll listen.' She pressed, if anything, more tightly against him.

Briefly, Marin outlined a route for her private hopjet to follow, where she should switch to her first Taxi-Air, and where she should finally make contact with a military transport.

'That's clever,' Delindy said thoughtfully when he had finished. 'Do you think it will really fool people?'

Marin explained the principles of deception. 'You're dealing with human beings, usually a limited number. They're handicapped by their need for secrecy. They get held up by crowds. If they get too far behind, they lose track of you.'

She seemed to accept that because she whispered, 'Oh, David, it's so good to be near you again. I've missed you so. I—' Her voice broke. The next second Marin had a sobbing woman in his arms. 'Oh, my dear,' she whispered. 'I'm so unhappy. How could such a thing have happened to us?'

Marin held her close. He had a sense of being shut down inside, as if his mind were not functioning, as if some quick-spring of his being were affected by the sound of her grief. He thought finally, in anguish, 'I can't let this affect me. This mustn't influence my decisions.'

And he didn't quite know what he meant by this.

Because – what decisions?

His only job was to become David Marin again – in fact, and not just in appearance.

The woman in his arms stopped crying abruptly. 'I'd better go,' she said. 'I'll see you at Rocket Take-Off.' She kissed him lightly and then rolled away from him; he heard the movement of her getting to her feet, and the sound of footsteps on the carpet. Then the door opened, and shut.

Marin lay for a while remembering the moments of her presence, the touch of her hands on his body, her whispering voice, her tears – all gone now, but not forgotten.

As the daughter of the former Jorgian ambassador, she was highly suspect. He could guess that her wanting to go to the Jorgian border was solely and only a test, to see if he would take her. She was, not improbably, trying to find out if this time it was to be war. Marin turned on his side, profoundly unhappy again over this wasted night.

His bedside clock showed eighteen minutes after one when he awakened with the decision firm in his mind. He climbed out of the bed and dressed in the darkness.

He did not review his decision to take action. That cycle had been completed while he slept restlessly. Without hesitation, he left the cabin and a moment later was heading toward the Great Judge's residence.

Marin walked along a pathway, pretending to be casual, pretending to be out for a walk. If Delindy could steal out to see him, then the reverse action was also possible.

He was, he realized, assuming absolutely that the entrance to the Shelters — formerly given the code number 808-B — *was* somewhere inside the Great Judge's cottage. Tonight would end all conjecture about that. And he would also determine for himself what was in the Shelters beneath these grounds. As soon as he got below surface, he would look quickly, and as thoroughly as time allowed.

As soon as . . .

That was the problem, of course. Getting in, getting down. Feeling helpless, Marin paused in the darkness of an overhanging shrub. Standing there, he forced the doubt out of his mind. There could be no turning back. If the Brain was down there in the Shelters, then tonight might be his only chance to find out.

From the shadows, he located himself in relation to the gardens. He knew this entire area. He had come about two hundred feet. Which meant: from the next cross path he would be able to see the Great Judge's residence.

Everything would be unlocked. That was the law. And on this level, the dictator obeyed his own decrees. It was the kind of thing that visitors looked for. On such small observances, the popularity of a leader depended.

For Marin, the alternatives for action were immensely simple. He could enter the house slyly by a devious fashion. Or . . .

Confidently, though quietly, Marin stode to the front door, softly opened it, stepped inside, and carefully closed the door behind him. He stood on the threshold in a darkness that was vaguely illuminated from a hallway to his right. And presently, when there was no sound, he felt a glee, a wild exhilaration, a thrill that was too heady, too abnormal, for his own good. It was the excitement of a man who had taken a great gamble with his own life as the stake.

And won.

. . . Not the first time. But never before like this, with *everything* involved – his life, his name, his position, his power. And what was doubly tensing was that the second step of the gamble, with the stakes the same, was already in process.

He tiptoed across the room, alert to the slightest touch of a stray piece of furniture. He knew this room from having been in it for conferences on cool nights. And so headed for a door directly opposite the main entrance. He found himself presently in a pitch-black hallway. And knew that beyond were the bedrooms – Delindy's to the right, the Great Judge's to the left.

It was impossible to see whether or not the bedroom doors were open. Marin waited. But there was no sound. And so he guessed, with relief, that the doors were closed. In the darkness, he fumbled over the wall to his right, located the elevator button, and pressed it.

Long ago, he had surmised that the presence of an elevator in a one-story bungalow meant either of two things: a basement, or – more likely – entrance 808-B to the Shelters. It was only natural that the Great Judge should have a quick way of escape in an emergency.

There was a soft hissing sound, and then a soft gliding sound. And then a glare of light as the elevator door slid open. Marin shuddered as that light flooded the hallway and as its reflections stirred the darkness of the large room he had just come through. But he held himself where he was. And, as the elevator door opened wide, stepped inside.

Once there, he shivered again. But this time with relief. The control panel was a combination type, with eleven buttons – 0 to 9, and a release. Like an electrically operated calculation machine, it could be set for any number of floors.

Marin set it for a hundred, and then pressed the release.

The door glided shut. The machine's mechanism hissed gently. Swiftly the elevator descended. There was a flickering

74

of light on the numbered buttons. From one to nine, the light was white. At ten, two numbers began to flash – the zero was white, the one red. For eleven, the one button registered red on its left half and white on the right half. At one hundred, as the elevator came to a halt, the one turned blue and the zero was red and white.

The door slipped open, and Marin had a narrow view of a typically drab corridor of the Shelters. He walked, blaster in hand; and on that level he spent just over half an hour, searching – if glancing into large, empty, concrete chambers, and along dark corridors could be called searching. He went down another level, then up two, then down four, and so on.

He walked with a developing sense of bafflement and never noticed when a sliding door opened behind and above him, revealing a flexible metal rod which took aim at him, and fired – something.

He walked on, was turned aside by a voice, which spoke to him from a hidden machine, and presently he was lying on a metal turntable. His perception was totally shut off at this point, and there was only a whispering of mechanical things – a faint hum, a sound as of someone tittering softly, portions of electronic thinking mechanisms 'talking' to each other.

No words were spoken, but records were made of brain vibrations, a brief study of his thought processes, and finally three control units impressed on the neural structure of the brain itself.

Then he was released.

Marin continued walking, without ever knowing that his search had been interfered with. Shortly before 5.00 A.M., weary, and convinced that no one man could ever more than begin to explore the Shelters, he took the elevator to the surface.

Again, though – oddly – not so strongly, he felt the tension of imminent discovery. But nothing occurred. And presently he was out in the garden. Then he was a hundred feet from the dictator's bungalow and knew that at very least he was safe from immediate exposure.

He crept into bed in the dim light of dawn. And the unhappiness over the wasted night was back. He kept waking, and each time the feeling was there, unchanged. He had somehow missed the truth, and therefore he had taken a profoundly dangerous risk and gained nothing.

. . . Wasted. . . .

Breakfast with the Great Judge was uneventful. They did not talk of the Jorgian war.

Shortly after breakfast Marin winged away from the Judge's Court.

As he removed the Marin disguise from the face and body of Wade Trask, he could mentally list only two things that had occurred during his visit. The Great Judge had listened to his plea on behalf of Wade Trask. And Delindy had secretly come to him to arrange the details of her going with him to Asia.

It seemed to him, who could leave nothing to chance, that either event could have been the main reason for his being invited to Court. He could well imagine that the conversation of the previous evening had been promoted by the Great Judge himself, and not by Edmund Slater. And Delindy's coming to him had three possible explanations. On the one hand the Great Judge might be coolly using his own mistress to spy on her former lover, clearly confident that she would be loyal to the ruler of a planet rather than to some underling. On the other hand, Delindy herself might be a Jorgian spy using her body, first to ensnare a Group Master, and then the dictator, for her own country. The third possibility was that she loved David Marin.

There was actually, Marin realized, a fourth consideration that he could have. She was a pawn of the Brain, unconsciously doing that mechanical being's work and consciously just being whatever she normally was.

Uneasily, Marin put that thought away from him. Not that it didn't have substance or meaning. It was simply too bizarre and out of his control.

It was not something he should think about on the morning of this third day, when there was so much else to be done.

CHAPTER EIGHTEEN

Marin opened the door of Trask's apartment and entered. The big room was bright with the brilliance of the morning. For just a moment he had the feeling it was unoccupied. And then Riva Allen arose from a corner chair. She uttered a cry of pleasure and plunged aggressively forward into his arms.

She wiggled, and twisted, and kissed, and squirmed with excitement. And then she seemed to remember something, drew back, and said in a subdued voice, 'I have instructions from Mr. Arallo that either you or I should call him the moment you came in.'

Marin said, 'Oh!'

Just like that, the day seemed less his own.

For a few moments, then, he had a strange, intense awareness of this world around him. There was first of all this very private room, Trask's apartment by right of lease – in effect, a private property, his castle where theoretically no one could damage him except under law. And then there was Trask's legal right to freedom until the hour of his execution. Yet, despite these rights, encroachments were possible on his time. His actions could be interfered with in a thousand ways; and therefore it was vitally important that he conform in some minimum fashion to the desires of all these intruding authorities.

He guessed that Arallo would not be happy about his disappearance for a day, felt briefly a Group Master's arrogance toward such underlings as Arallo and then remembered his circumstances. No use avoiding the issue.

He pressed a connecting button. 'Arallo, Tilden!' he said in a clear voice.

Clarity of pronunciation was necessary for the electronic devices that completed the call for him on the basis of the sound of the name alone. A development of Trask Electronics from previously known methods, the equipment involved was still limited mostly to government officials. Trask had only this one unit in his apartment. The button activated a servo-mechanism, which was then ready to record his words when he spoke them; another mechanism made a graph of the electrical impulse created by the sound. A scanner next examined the graph, classified it as belonging to a certain group of sounds. A servo-mechanism rejected all other groups, and a scanner looked over three-dimensional plastic models of the graph – which had been previously constructed – and selected one that represented Tilden Arallo from a score or so of similar words. Another servo-mechanism, in series, selected another three-dimensional plastic model, this one representing a phone number, and the process was carried through to the point where still another servo-mechanism electrically dialed the desired number. A similar technique was used for automatic language translation and for speaking directly into a typewriter.

There was a tiny pause while the intricate process was completed. A wall screen switched on, and a man's face appeared on it. Tilden Arallo said from the screen, 'Oh, it's you, Trask.'

He seemed unfriendly, not cheerful, though brisk. His brows were knit, his lips pursed and his eyes grave. He looked like a man with problems. Marin said in a mild tone, 'Riva said you wanted to speak to me.'

Arallo nodded. 'I want to remind you that tonight is regular group meeting night.'

Marin said nothing. It seemed clear, from the other's manner, that Trask's disappearance for a day *had* put him out of favour with the group. He waited.

Arallo went on. 'We expect you to be in attendance.'

'I can see no reason why not,' said Marin.

'Frankly, neither can I,' said Arallo. He hesitated; then: 'I would advise a spirit of friendly communication.' With that he broke the connection.

Marin sat silent. Arallo's attitude seemed to foreshadow future difficulties, which might affect him seriously. And yet, there was little that he could do. Real communication was out of the question. He dismissed the matter. He turned, and said to Riva, 'I have things to do in my study, and I don't wish to be disturbed.'

He was about to turn away when he realized from her expression that he was being too abrupt. He said, 'I'll be free tonight, my dear.'

She shook her head and said bitterly, 'You can't fool me. You're dead already.'

But she pushed him toward the study door. 'All right, get your work done. Would you like me to make lunch?'

'Yes,' said Marin, relieved at her co-operation.

Nevertheless, as he closed the study door, he was surprised to realize that he was trembling. He wasted no time exploring the feeling but hastily braced the door shut with a chair, and, opening the hidden entrance to the laboratory, went inside.

The glitter of glass, the sheen of instruments, the long gleaming table – that was the impact on his eyes. And on the floor . . .

One look was all Marin needed. The body – *his* – was conscious.

He walked over to it and looked down at his captive. The bound man's eyes studied him anxiously, yet with irritation rather than fear.

Marin said, 'Can you hear me?'

The man on the floor jiggled his head. yes.

Marin said, 'I want you to tell me where you took your invention when you removed it from Trask Laboratories, after you left me.'

His answer was a slight, cynical smile, then a shake of the head. And then he tried to spit out the gag.

Marin bent down and, with a recollection of how strong his own teeth had always been, warily removed the gag. He knelt, then, ready to clamp the gag on again. Curious, he asked, 'How did you happen to trap yourself?'

The other man looked at him gloomily. 'Now that you're close up I see you're not wearing my glasses.'

Marin had almost forgotten the episode of taking off the glasses. Now a light dawned. He waited.

'It happened suddenly,' Trask said in a tense tone. 'I was here getting some equipment, when – just like that – my vision gave out. I stumbled against the back of the clock and must have short-circuited a wire, because I got a shock that knocked me out. It was one of those damned accidents.'

He seemed depressed by the memory. Marin scarcely noticed. An accident! Had the same accident triggered a connection which resulted in strands of luminescence reaching out from the clock face into the bedroom toward his bed on that first night?

If that were true, it meant a further delay of explanations in an area where there was far too little certainty as it was.

Trask was speaking, in a hushed tone, 'David, can't you see that this is the biggest thing that ever was? In just that one aspect of vision you and I have changed the science of psychology.'

Marin shrugged. He felt cold to this argument. 'Psychology is not a science,' he said flatly. 'You can only have opinions on it, and one group never accepts the opinions of another. We stopped using psychologists in the armed forces, except as minor technicians under the direction of soldiers.'

Trask seemed not to have heard. 'How long . . .' he said in a tense voice, 'how long did it take? To get your vision back, I mean?'

'About fifteen hours,' said Marin curtly.

'The same time as myself,' Trask said triumphantly. In spite of his bonds, he sat up. 'David, don't you see what this means? It's the attitude a person has that counts, his philosophy. Ever since I can remember, I've held myself away from the world of action. I've been the thinker looking on – from a safe distance. The scientist, observer, the spectator. And my eyes took on the nearsighted shape from that behaviour pattern.'

It was briefly interesting to Marin that this man could at this tremendous period of his life become scientifically excited over oddities of his invention. It seemed to make him more human. He felt himself thawing – not much, but a little.

He said gently, 'Trask, where did you take the invention? I want it.'

The excitement faded out of the other's eyes. He gazed at Marin somberly. 'David, we're partners now, whether you like it or not. Don't you see that?'

Marin shook his head. 'You do exactly as I say. That's what I see.'

'All I have to do,' said Trask, 'is do nothing, and you go to the Converter four days from now. That puts me in a strong bargaining position.' The fine, dark eyes that looked up at Marin were slightly narrowed, as if they were searching for a clue to Marin's purposes.

Marin said, 'I have no time to argue. Every obstacle you place in my way will make me less inclined to help you . . .

later. I repeat, and this is the last time I ask! Where's the equipment?'

Trask stared at him, and suddenly he looked shaken. 'You damned scoundrel!' he half sobbed. 'I know that tone of voice. I recognize a killer when I hear one. But you couldn't damage your own body.'

Marin waited. He had killed, as an instrument of government. He would undoubtedly do so again. By assuming that what a man would do as a government agent was the same as what he would do for personal reasons, Trask was talking himself into fear.

'Look,' said Trask desperately, 'if I had time I could convince you that this combination group and free-enterprise idea has as many flaws as each system separately.' He must have believed Marin was about to interrupt, for he went on with breathless speed: 'David, if we were seeking superman, we would have to begin with the willingness to face death at any instant. And so, the first place we look for data is an army on the move. There we see an incredible phenomenon – men at the peak of their strength trained to fight to the death.

'Whenever a leader of genius sees that, he has a heady feeling about the potential power of human beings. He can visualize masses of men organized to achieve great goals. In practice, this doesn't seem to work out. Take a man out of the military establishment, and he loses the greatness that derives from the association. Five thousand years of fighting have proved that army life is not the way to the self-sufficient person who yet recognizes his interdependence with other people.'

He paused, feeling unhappy. 'I can see I'm not making much headway,' he confessed. 'You're loyal to the Great Judge and—' He broke off. 'David, have you ever asked yourself where the Great Judge came from? What is his background? Now, please don't give me the stereotyped answers, the publicity and the official history. Born in that part of the Soviet now known as Jorgia, brought up in an engineer's home, became an army officer. Not that part. Have you ever seen an account that bridged the gap between Colonel Ivan Prokov and the Great Judge? Frankly, I haven't, and I like my life stories to have continuity.'

Marin said patiently, 'I can give you the data. It was a very fluid period in the Combined Eastern Powers armed forces. Late in the war, the Russian field officers realized what the general staff officers seemed not to know: that the common soldier was just about through. Led by Colonel Ivan Prokov, they—'

He stopped, because Trask was gazing at him satirically. 'You know your catechism, don't you? But, my friend, just how does that explain a man who was nearly fifty years old twenty-five years ago and now looks thirty-eight?'

He gave Marin a searching look. 'Do you have any comment?' he asked.

Marin hesitated. He was not disposed to pursue this discussion, which he regarded as fruitless. But he was recalling the period when he was first adjusting to Trask's body. The dream-like memories – that scene where what was evidently a dying man was asking for help. The incident could well be a clue to the mystery of Trask's past associations.

He described the scene to Trask briefly and said, 'I gathered that he could have the help only if he could tell why he was ill. What happened to him?'

Trask said, 'One of my early experiments in self-sufficiency.'

'What did the experiment prove?'

The other man was scowling. 'This is a lame-duck world, David. A large percentage of people are so deeply involved in the need for someone to tell them what to do, think, feel and believe that they will die rather than become aware of their *own* responsibility for illness, failure and other disabilities. We've got to change that. We've got to set up a system where people are interdependent, and where an authority on some subject is merely a source of information for his equals.'

'This man died?'

'No.' Trask shrugged. 'After he fell into a coma, we fulfilled our role of father or mother substitute and saved him.'

Marin nodded. He had one more question before coming to his main point: 'Where did these experiments occur?'

'In Jorgia. The Queen and her then teen-age sister encouraged all kinds of experiments in living, and since they didn't ask too many questions, I moved to Jorgia and lived there for three years.'

'During those three years,' said Marin, 'who were you associated with?'

Trask gave him a searching look, then shrank a little. 'You're after something,' he muttered uneasily. 'I can see that. But I'll tell you anyway. Some of the finest people I've ever met. Idealists, perhaps. But they recognized the value of my ideas on how people should live together. They encouraged me to experiment.'

Curious, Marin asked, 'How did you meet these people?'

'I met two men and a woman at college. We used to talk for hours. Of course, I didn't have the ideas perfected then.'

Marin persisted: 'Did you go to Jorgia immediately after university?'

'No. Not until after I had developed the resonance device with the infinite-series echo chamber that made possible undistorted round-the-world radio and television transmission. That gave me all the money I needed. I was free to pursue further studies.'

'You sought these people out then?'

Trask hesitated. Then, irritably: 'Now, look, I'm trying to be completely honest. But this is all irrelevant. I'll be glad to tell you all about it someday.'

Marin nodded. 'All right. But two more questions first.'

'All right.' Trask seemed resigned.

Marin asked, 'Were there many of these . . . idealists . . . in Jorgia?'

'I met about two hundred,' said Trask. 'I had the impression there were thousands.' He added, 'They seemed to know people from everywhere.'

'Question two,' said Marin. 'Did you tell them about your identity-shifting invention?'

Trask shook his head. 'Not directly.'

'How do you mean?'

'Well . . .' The scientist looked unhappy. 'I did hint that I was working on something big. But I evaded their questions about it.'

'Why?'

'Well . . .' Trask was suddenly thoughtful. 'I can see what you're getting at. Why didn't I trust them, if they were so worth while? I think it was my inventor's secrecy complex, and also I thought a few of them were a little on the violent side. I could imagine those individuals trying to force a change, and frankly I felt that the inventor of a history-making invention ought to have some say as to its use and influence.' He laughed harshly. 'I didn't realize how soon I would be forced to act at breakneck speed.'

'A little too breakneck, evidently,' said Marin grimly.

But he was enormously relieved at the information Trask had given him. He had a partial picture of the situation now. Trask was a peculiar mixture of genuine idealism and practical understanding of life. The group that had gotten hold of him had found him mentally so tough that they had not even attempted to indoctrinate him with their own ideas. He was certainly not in their confidence, nor even a member of their organization. They had played him on a long line, giving him plenty of room to maneuver.

Trask was speaking. 'David,' he said earnestly, 'you don't realize how far we've gotten away from the idea that a human being has a right to recognition of his innate personal dignity. Reduced to its simplest elements, the idea is: If you violate the rights of one person, you violate the rights of all. I subscribe to that.'

Marin said, 'I gather that this body-switching trick which you have played on me is not a violation of your code.'

There was a pause. It was clearly a point that, in the intensity of making his argument, Trask had forgotten. He said finally, slowly, 'This is a great crisis in my life. A man who has invented an instrument that will alter the history of the human race provides a special situation.'

He stopped. The expression on his face seemed to say that his own words had surprised him into a new thought. His face was suddenly wet with perspiration.

Momentarily, then, Marin remembered that it was *his* body feeling, tensing, perspiring, as the beingness of Trask experienced one thought after another. It seemed like a desecration, a soiling of that once strong, healthy body.

Then Trask was speaking; and the fantastic reality of transposed bodies yielded before the meaning of his words. He whispered hoarsely, 'David, you won't have to use torture. I'll give you the invention. I'll show you how to use it.'

CHAPTER NINETEEN

Marin waited. He was astonished, and not convinced. Men facing eternity had roughly three reactions: they were calm and frozen; or wild or emotional (with many variations); or good-humored. Those last were usually total partisans of an opposing philosophy. They had gambled and lost, and they accepted their fate with a joke and a twisted smile.

Trask was beginning to act like one of the emotional ones. He said grimly, 'The moment you have control of the invention, you will stand at a crossroad of history, able to make over the world according to your views. Therefore, you will have no alternative but to act exactly as I did.'

Abruptly calm and resigned, he looked up at his captor. 'You'll kill me, of course – later.' He spoke musingly. 'Although that depends. Maybe you can use me.'

It was such a different and more compelling Trask that, just for an instant, Marin looked into the direction at which the other's words pointed. And then, shaken, he wouldn't look any more.

. . . Treason, personal ambition, revenge impulses – that was the view. Ideals, also, of course, but they were vague.

He said stiffly, 'It is a tenet of the group idea that a man must voluntarily subordinate himself for the good of the group.'

Trask grinned. He seemed to be completely free again, within himself. He said, 'David, the group idea isn't big enough and basic enough to get that kind of loyalty from an individual. The only force that can do it is the individual's conviction that he is a permanent entity within the framework of eternity.'

Marin said, 'Oh, so it's the back-to-God movement.'

Trask remained cheerful. 'I didn't say that. I merely made a logical statement.'

Despite the surface good nature, he must have been nettled, for he broke off. 'The invention is in your hopjet.' He spoke curtly.

Marin stared at him, and he thought, Of course.

It was the most likely location, and one which perhaps he

would have guessed at sooner or later. What could be a more inviolable hiding place than a Group Master's private plane. And, of course, Trask – flying in the machine to his laboratory – would not, could not, take into account that a minor accident, a stumble, would plunge him from the height of potential power to disaster.

Marin didn't have to be told where to look in the plane. It would be the luggage compartment.

'Bring it in here,' said Trask.

Marin did not move. 'Then what?' he asked.

'Everything is here,' said Trask. 'Enough power and the necessary connecting units.'

Marin was somber. 'You won't mind,' he said, 'if I also bring along a lie detector.'

Trask shrugged. 'It's not necessary, but suit yourself.'

'And,' asked Marin, 'if I gag you while I'm out?'

'It's not necessary,' said Trask, 'but go ahead.' He added, 'The walls between these apartments have been sound-proofed from each other, and the laboratory from the rest of the apartment.'

Marin was inclined to believe him. But truth was not really an issue. It was that he could take no chances. At this point, Trask, if freed in any way, could prove he was David Marin.

And David Marin, looking like Trask, would not survive by more than a few hours the discovery that he had imprisoned what appeared to be a Group Master.

He fitted the gag in place and then went out into the apartment. Riva sat curled up on a divan, reading. She threw the book aside and jumped up.

'Through?' she asked eagerly.

'Just beginning,' said Marin quickly. And then, from the door, he added over his shoulder, 'I'm bringing some equipment in from my plane. Be back in a few minutes.'

There were three boxes in the luggage compartment of the hopjet. Marin carried them in one at a time and set them down in the den. Then he disconnected the lie detector from the special instrument section of the very special control board of his machine and carried it also into his den.

In the laboratory again, he set up Trask's invention, under the bound man's direction. Then, using the lie detector, he asked pointed questions, the answers to which established beyond doubt that Trask was actually handing over his invention.

He forced himself to stop finally. He stood, then, tense, excited, and jumped with anxiety as the great living-room clock vibrated – the faint sound of it striking the noon hour came through to him.

It cost him an effort, but he went out to the kitchen.

Lunch with Riva was highly disturbing to Marin, for he attempted to be lighthearted. And the nervous charge in him would not let him be still. Twice he told jokes; and each time laughed until the tears rolled down his cheeks, and the startled girl gazed at him in amazement, her own quick laughter stifled by surprise and wonder.

Marin returned to the laboratory sobered by his own antics. And now he wasted not a moment. Without warning, he fired a timed gas charge into the body on the floor. The moment it went limp, he untied the bonds, removed the gag, and stretched the still form on the floor beside the machine. Swiftly he attached the electrodes – eight on one side and nearly a score on the other; each one over an important nerve center.

He'd been a little startled at some of the nerve centers Trask considered important. The principal joints: knees, hips, ankles, wrists, shoulders, the base of the throat, small of the back, just left of the heart, the sides of the head, top center of the head and the two temples.

A few of the connections went through a servo-mechanism, which was neatly constructed, to revive or render unconscious either Trask or himself, depending on how it was set.

It took time for the next step – the laborious task of attaching the wires to his own body. Ready at last, he lay down beside the other body, reached for the activator, and paused.

He thought grimly, Have I made any errors? He felt hot and afraid. If he had, if he failed now, then he might not have another opportunity.

He forced his body to relax, hesitated a moment longer. And pressed the activator.

Several seconds went by but nothing happened.

Marin held himself calm, fighting a developing sense of dismay. After the tense indecision of the past forty-eight hours, his failure was a bitter anticlimax.

'Wait!' he told himself, 'give it time. After all, a human being *is* complex and probably responds slowly.'

He was still thinking that when a voice said right into his ears, 'Emergency report: power be now used by a not known unit.'

Marin jumped involuntarily and turned his head. The shock of that voice was throbbing inside him as he twisted his head and looked around wildly for the speaker. Except for the silent form, on the floor beside him, the laboratory was empty.

Before he could think about that, a second voice said, 'Directional find – did be find interfere unit – Group 814 area.'

There was a pause, and once more Marin gazed around the room. It was still deserted. His mind began to work. He thought, Why, they're speaking straight into my brain.

*Mental telepath*y. But how – what?

That was as far as he got. A third voice said, 'No contact be possible. Receiving unit be human person. Further operation command be now necessary and include more data.'

Other sensations – not verbal – were coming now. They seemed to be more on the level of automatic processes, partly below consciousness. Marin could feel a tugging at what seemed to be the base of his brain, and then, vaguely, stirrings inside his body: changes taking place, readjustments of functions, tiny manipulations of his glands and cells. The contact was as deep and thorough as that.

A new voice said, 'Communications unit 28658 report now. Intruder be accidentally connected, and be not attached to organization. Exterior action needing.'

The answer came: 'Central be have use now exterior servo-mechanisms.'

Marin, who had been following the dialogue with a developing amazement, convulsively pressed the button that deactivated his mechanism, and broke the connection with the unconscious body beside him. He sat up, and, in doing so, pulled off half a dozen of the electrodes that had been attached to his own skin. As he did so, the faint, now faraway voice of Communications said, 'Direct contact broken. Confusion of identity, though the name Wade Trask did now come through clearly. The other name be not ...' The voice – or whatever it was – faded abruptly and was gone.

Marin began shakily to detach the electrodes from the unconscious body beside him. Then he sank back on a table; and now his mind reached for the answer to the fantastic thing that had happened.

His attempt to switch back to his own body had failed.

That was a personal failure. It gave him a blank feeling about his future. But there was no mistaking the reason for the failure. The peculiar language that had impinged on his mind was the famous spoken Model English, used in the most advanced types of electronic thinking machines. And that meant . . .

The Brain was alive.

The impact of that vibrated down into him, and he was like a man who had had a sudden glimpse of a hidden reality. It was as if a fissure had opened for an instant in a green meadow, revealing the fire and violence of the volcanic core of a planet to the wondering eyes of a simple farmer.

Marin sagged for an indeterminate time considering the implications. He recalled what Slater had said about weird methods of mind-control by means of electronic circuits apparently impressed on the brain mass itself.

That had not happened here. But Trask was identified. Through him, Marin could be found. Which meant . . . what?

Marin groaned inwardly as he tied the still-unconscious body. Then he sat down to consider his next move.

He could, presumably, transfer himself to another body. Just what would eventually happen to the essence of a personality filtered through one nervous system after another was not clear. But he guessed he would, throughout, retain the identity feeling of David Marin. He himself had altered extravagantly in fifteen years, but it seemed like the same individuality.

Sitting there in the silence of the laboratory with his own body lying on the floor, Marin considered the possibility of using other bodies as a means of escape.

He shook his head finally, and forever dismissed it as a solution. It had a fateful flaw. It meant inflicting upon another human being the inheritance of death that went with the physical being of Wade Trask.

Without the initial data he had had, another person would surely go mad.

Schemes, feelings, determination, weakness, a terrible conviction of urgency, ended finally as he thought, I'll have to
wake Trask up. I need another brain on this.

He had no belief that Trask could provide him with an ultimate solution. But it would be someone to talk to, a new
viewpoint, new ideas.

Marin hesitated, and then fired the awakening gas charge
into the inert body on the floor.

A few moments later, Trask was stirring.

CHAPTER TWENTY

The man groaned a little, and twisted, as if he were in a state of
discomfort. His cheeks were pale under their tan. Once, his
eyes opened, and it was visibly an action that had no consciousness in it, and no sight. The eyelids flickered shut, and
then he lay still, stiffening slightly. Now there was no doubt.
Thought was coming. The next instant Trask sighed and
opened his eyes.

Marin waited. Such things as this could not be rushed,
particularly after the body had been unconscious several
times.

He waited. And then he began to talk. And all the while his
indecision was a continuing tension. He explained about the
'thing' in David Burnley's mind, and what Edmund Slater had
told him about the search for the Brain. He described what had
happened two nights before with the luminous 'rope'.

Trask, who had listened quietly till that instant, interrupted.
'You mean, you think I triggered that when I fell against the
back of the clock?'

'I have no idea,' said Marin. 'I'm telling you what occurred,
not why. Let me finish.'

Trask did not interrupt again. But his face had a strained
expression on it as Marin described what had happened when
he had tried to use the machine on the two of them a few hours
earlier.

He lay silent when Marin finally finished. Then he said
slowly, 'David, have you considered the implications of what I

did when I gave you my invention without asking anything from you in return?'

Marin, who had his own ideas on basic motives, said, 'How do you mean?'

'I did it because it was the logical thing to do.'

Marin shook his head slightly, but he knew what Trask meant – logical that he would be compelled by his personal power drive to do with the invention what Trask had planned to do. Since he had as yet had no such thought, Trask's logic was not as clearly reasonable as Trask believed. Still, the man had acted with decision. And it was a high-level action unmistakably involving the risk of death. Marin waited.

Trask went on, urgently. 'Can you be less logical? Release me.'

'*What!*'

He was astonished. His mind reached in every direction around the thought, considering ... that Trask *could* be confined and controlled by the fact that the Brain existed.

Marin thought, I could take all models of the invention. I could use my equipment to disguise him as Trask. Despite the man's immense know-how about things electronic, Trask would find it hard to break free of any 'set' of appearance forced upon him by that method. Many an alien spy, sent back as an agent, had had only that one factor of altered appearance to force him to act as an agent of the Great Judge.

Marin's thought wandered, then, for an instant. He had often speculated on the problems faced by such a spy, returned to his own country, looking like someone else, not daring to reveal himself, and with an activated pain circuit imprinted on his muscles as a constant reminder of what was expected of him. Such a man would not be in half the peculiar situation of Wade Trask in Marin's body, disguised as Trask; and Marin disguised as Marin.

If the whole affair were not so deadly, it would be incredibly funny.

He visualized Trask free, and that seemed complicated and dangerous. He said slowly, 'I don't follow your reasoning.'

But he felt shaken, and indecisive, and half convinced.

Trask said tensely, 'David, we can't waste my talent and training in this situation. The Brain is an electronic computer,

91

and that's my field. No one now living knows more than I do in that area. You need me as much as I need you. Don't you see?'

'I see you free, betraying me.'

'How?' Trask's tone was both pleading and impatient. 'For heaven's sake, David, I need you desperately. I can't afford to betray you. Listen . . .' And he outlined precautions Marin could take, exactly as Marin had thought them. Control of the invention. Disguise of the Marin body . . .

Trask paused there, and said, 'I presume you will not at this moment consider making the switch-over anyway, Brain or no Brain.'

Marin said simply, 'Somebody has to be uncontrolled. I feel myself to be free at this moment.'

'Suppose the Great Judge is an agent of the Brain?'

Marin said warily, 'Yes? What then?'

'Would you still have to be loyal to him?' Trask broke off. 'Wait. Don't answer that. It's not at issue, at this stage. Sooner or later you'll come face to face with that. But right now we have things to do that will be valuable regardless of ultimate choices.'

Marin nodded. He was accustomed to operate within strict frames of reference. He said cautiously, 'If I released you, what would prevent you from building a copy of your invention and becoming the Great Judge, as you originally planned?'

'Would you care to have me answer that, with the lie detector?'

Marin wasted not a moment but attached that telltale instrument; and Trask said, 'I couldn't duplicate it in less than three weeks.'

The lie detector verified the statement.

It was, Marin realized, the decisive moment. And it was too quick. There were several things he must do first.

'No,' he said. 'Not yet. Later.'

'Why not?' Trask visibly held his anger.

Marin shook his head. 'I've got to get the invention out of here. And, besides, frankly, I've got to think over what I should really do with a man as dangerous as you.'

Trask moaned softly in dismay. 'You fool,' he said. 'For heaven's sake, man, don't delay. We have so little time. Even this one extra evening might be decisive.'

Marin hesitated. He had an intuition that Trask was right. But he was also remembering the phone call the previous morning. He said, 'What's your relation with Ralph Scudder?'

A startled look flashed over the other's face. Trask swallowed hard, and then he said lamely, 'Scudder – you mean, the Pripp?'

Marin gazed down at the disconcerted man and shook his head. 'I don't have time right now to ask you any questions about Scudder. . . .'

Trask recovered. 'For heaven's sake, man, Scudder is just someone who furnished me with experimental subjects a year ago. I was hoping I could make some use of his organization. Nothing is settled. I was supposed to meet him again. He's suspicious, but greedy. It was a shock to realize you knew about it, that's all. I felt as if my life line were threatened.'

'I see.' Marin believed the story. But he shook his head decisively. 'There are too many uncontrolled factors here,' he said. 'For instance, it's group meeting for you tonight. I hate to spend the time, but I have an idea it will be safer for both of us if I attend for you. At least then I'll know how much of a problem there is in that territory.' He broke off decisively. 'I'll come back afterward, and I'll commit myself one way or another. I promise.'

He glanced at his watch. 'I'll have time to eat, sneak some food in here for you, get the invention back on my hopjet, and be on my way.'

He had a strong sense of relief as he went out. He still couldn't quite visualize Trask free. The scientist had gone so deep into treason that – it seemed to Marin – to associate with him in any way other than that of captor and captive would be ultimately compromising.

But there was another feeling that went along with that conviction. It was the feeling that great events were in the making and that he would act decisively before this night was over.

CHAPTER TWENTY-ONE

7:30 P.M.

It was a typical group meeting. Marin, as Trask, sat in chair 564, and received from the group numerous expressions of affinity for him as a human being without, as one speaker put it, 'in any way condoning those statements you made which were considered seditious.'

8:40 P.M. And still raining, as Marin emerged from the group center. The colored plate-glass windows, with their built-in lighting systems, cast reflections far out into the square – that symbol of the atomic age.

It was like being in a private world to be here surrounded by tall buildings, with only four exits, and those deliberately narrow and low built, like bridges – or tunnels – that speared through the overhanging mass of building at each corner.

Marin scarcely noticed. He was trying to make up his mind: Go to see Scudder at ten o'clock, or . . .

He had a time-consuming job to do. He needed to study old reports on the Shelters. What *had* happened to the area where, later, the residence of the Great Judge had been constructed? It might be days before he'd have the necessary time, whereas he *could* call Scudder at ten and suggest a meeting at eleven-thirty. That was what he decided to do.

He went, disguised as Marin, to his own headquarters. For nearly two hours confidential clerks scurried from file cabinets to his desk. There was the smell of dust and of old paper – but in the end he had some facts.

The Shelters had been particularly badly damaged in that section. A bomb had freakishly punched a hole nearly half a mile deep and hundreds of yards in diameter at that precise location. The Brain *could* have been lowered into such an unusual indentation and covered up by subsequent construction – provided the Great Judge gave the necessary orders.

As he left the office, Marin thought, grayly, I keep coming back to that.

CHAPTER TWENTY-TWO

Still raining. The darkness above his hopjet was like pitch. He headed for Pripp City.

There was no interference. His machine glided lower, nearer, to the improbable community that soon spread in all directions beneath him.

Marin walked along the street, observing the cruel pranks that fate had played. The phenomena both repelled and fascinated him; for this was on the level of the cell, or rather in the energy zone below the molecular band – the level where his invention operated. He had had plans and theories about what might be done with and for Pripps.

His mind poised there. Because that was not *his* thought.

He himself had no scientific understanding of Trask's invention, nor had he ever had any plans for the Pripps.

He had a sudden, intense sense of uneasiness. To have had the other man's memories surge up again in so subtle a fashion was somehow unsettling. It seemed to prove that there was conflict below the level of his awareness. The suppressed memories of Trask were seeking an outlet. Was it possible that the Trask beingness might suddenly surge up and take over?

The keyed-up feeling stayed with Marin as he entered a phone-booth and called Pleasure, Incorporated.

A woman answered. After he had identified himself, she said, 'Two individuals will meet you on level three of the Shelters in ten minutes. That's via sub entrance eight. Submit yourself entirely to their directions. They will take you to Mr. Scudder.'

Marin waited.

'Sub-entrance eight to the Shelters,' continued the woman, 'is a hundred yards westward from where you are now calling.'

'I'll be there,' said Marin.

Level three was a poorly lighted steel cavern. Vague lights receded into the distance in either direction along the corridor, and here and there – as he walked slowly in the direction he had been told to – Marin came to cross corridors where the lights were even more distantly spaced. A great silence lay over everything.

Two figures appeared finally far along that dim main hallway. Marin continued to walk toward them. He saw that they were a male and a female.

'My name is Yischa,' said the male Pripp. 'Dan Yischa.' He did not introduce the woman.

He added, 'Before we go on – a question.'

Marin said, 'Yes?'

In the dim light, the male Pripp said, 'You once used Pripps as experimental subjects because of our genetic memory. Do you need more such subjects, and, if so, will either of us fulfill your requirements?'

Marin parted his lips to reject the offer. But he was bemused by the meaning of the other's words. And so he closed them again because— Was it possible he could make use of these people? He said finally, out of curiosity, 'What can you remember?'

There was a pause; then: 'I have all memory; the memory of racial beginnings. Is that what you wish?'

Was that true? Marin wondered.

He realized with a curious tense excitement that with Trask's invention he could become a Pripp and find out. Just what he would do with the information was another matter. But the great thought was: It was possible. At last, man could explore the full meaning of life and also the terrible game it had played in creating the Pripps.

Again, stronger than before, came the thought: What can I do with this – now?

He had the feeling that he ought to have the two individuals handy, just in case something occurred to him.

Marin motioned to the girl. 'What about her?' he asked.

He did not address the girl directly, for Pripp women had collapsed to a lower psychological level than Pripp men. As a result, they were regarded as pawns – even by themselves.

Yischa turned to the woman. 'What can you remember?' he asked threateningly.

'The sea,' she said, in a sad voice, and shivered under the light. 'The slime of ocean bottoms. Rocks in deep water. Hot beaches, and no escape ever from the burning sun.'

Yischa turned to Marin. 'Does that comply with your requirements?' he asked politely.

Marin was abruptly decisive. 'I want you both for an experiment,' he said.

'Dangerous?'

'You won't be hurt physically.'

That seemed to be all that counted. 'Pay?'

'Two hundred dollars each.'

'Where do we report?'

Marin gave Trask's address. 'I want you to call me there about 1:00 A.M. tonight.'

He took out his billfold and handed two fifty-dollar bills to the girl, who stood near him. 'There's fifty each,' he said.

The girl hastily put one of the bills in the bosom of her dress and held the other out to her companion. 'One's mine,' she said. Her voice trembled.

Yischa snatched what she held out and moved as if he would attack her. With an effort he restrained himself. But he was trembling as he said, 'We'll have to blindfold you, sir.'

They looked like two gargoyles, figures out of a world of masks, the woman's face catlike, the man's peculiarly human, with an overlay of fox, or even dog.

It was not the moment to object. Blindfolded, Marin walked. It was a long walk that ended inside an elevator going up; then more walking, then another elevator going down. A door opened. Somebody snatched at the blindfold. Simultaneously, rough hands grabbed him. The next instant a brilliant light flashed into Marin's eyes.

A man's voice said, 'Search him!'

It was a vaguely familiar voice, and though he had only heard it in a phone conversation, Marin guessed that it was Scudder talking. Even as he had the thought, hands were probing into his pockets. He felt the motion when his gas guns were pulled out. The hands let go.

In spite of the dazzling light, Marin could see now. He was in a large office, with half a dozen Pripps, big fellows, except for Scudder, small, ratlike, malignant, who sat behind the single large desk in the room.

Scudder said, 'All right, that pulls your teeth. Now we can talk without my having to worry about your doing something against me.'

Marin, who had recovered wholly, shrugged. 'Oh, come now,

Ralph . . .' The first name came hard, but he used it. 'You don't think I'd try anything against a man who might help me?'

Scudder seemed to hesitate. 'With anyone else that would make sense,' he said at last, slowly. 'But, Wade, you know too much about the Pripps. I got reports on the experiments you performed, and I can't figure what you did there. I had a feeling I might be used whether I liked it or not.'

Marin said earnestly, 'I'm here, Ralph, because I have something you might be able to use – to both our benefits.'

But he was thinking with tense excitement. 'What plans Trask must have had. Using these strange beings – the Pripps.'

Marin said aloud, 'I'd like to talk to you in private. It won't require but a few minutes.'

Scudder had apparently reassured himself completely, for, at his command, his bodyguard trooped out of the room.

And they were alone. . . .

The little man sat behind his big desk, a humanlike creature, with a shrewd brain and full of the bitter humors of the mistreated, yet he smiled as he said, 'You've got three days left, not counting tonight. I don't know why I'm even giving you my time.'

'I've been thinking,' said Marin.

Scudder said, with a note of respect, 'I have an odd feeling about you, Wade. There's genius in those gray cells of yours. I'm willing to listen, though I can't figure what you can do in three days.'

It was an impressive tribute. But in spite of the encouragement, Marin hesitated. The idea he was going to introduce was so big it needed a build-up, so that the impact of the final revelation would hit this little man with full force.

'Ralph,' he began, 'you've explored the whole of the Shelters?'

It seemed to him that Scudder paused a moment before answering. 'Yes.' The Pripp leader spoke softly. He added, 'In a way.'

'About how much of it is sealed off?'

The Pripp looked at him with bright eyes. 'Three quarters,' he said, and added, 'That's a rough guess, of course.'

Marin persisted. 'And how much of that three quarters do you control?'

Scudder shook his head. 'I think you're on the wrong track, friend. I control only a small part – one twentieth at most. There's actually an entire section where we don't even go.'

Marin made his first big leap, mentally. He said, 'Ralph, how many people have you lost, trying to penetrate that area?'

There was silence. The bright eyes regarded him enigmatically. But they seemed to glisten with an inner excitement. His answer, when it came, was an evasion: 'We were told not to go there. I sent men anyway. They never came back.'

'Not one?'

'Not one.'

Marin sighed. And the tension in him grew stronger. For there must have been determination in this strange creature-man to have sent so many of his agents to their doom.

Marin said, 'Any clues as to why?'

'None.' The bright eyes glittered with the beginning of impatience.

Marin refused to be hurried. 'Who told you to remain out of that area?'

No answer.

Marin persisted. 'It was the Great Judge, wasn't it, Ralph?'

Scudder stood up abruptly. 'What are you getting at?' he asked curtly.

It was time for the impact.

'The Brain is hidden there, Ralph, and we've got to get to it, and control it, and tell it what we want it to do.'

The ratlike eyes of Ralph Scudder closed, and then they opened. And now he looked like some gleeful demon, alive with lecherous hope.

He said, and it was almost a whisper, 'Wade, you've done it. This is the biggest possibility I've heard in years. If this works out, you'll make it.'

He stood up, tense. 'What's the plan?'

Marin wasted no time now. 'I must have a map that will demarcate the boundaries of the forbidden area, above and below as well as on every side.'

Scudder pursed his thin lips. 'That seems simple enough. We kept records. I'll have a map drawn.'

'All right,' said Marin, 'that's it. That's what I wanted. How about having your blindfold boy come in and take me away?'

'Wait!' said Scudder.

He tapped with thin, clawlike fingers on his desk. He said finally, 'That's a fast interview, Wade. It's not like you. You're usually so careful. You've got every detail in your mind. Tell me something about the Brain.'

It was the first of more than a dozen questions, each one deliberate, each relevant – in a way – but actually merely irritating to Marin, who had no plan of value in connection with the Brain. In his replies, Marin gave mainly the information he had received from Slater. Since it seemed to be more than the Pripp gang leader possessed, it must have been satisfactory, because at last, after what seemed an interminable delay, Scudder said, 'I'll have Dan come in – and you'll get in touch with me.'

'Yes,' said Marin.

Scudder said, 'The day after tomorrow. Your last day. You're really cutting it close.'

Marin said, 'I have equally important things to do.'

Scudder said, 'I've got to hand it to you, Wade. But I sure wish I knew what you were up to.'

Marin said earnestly, 'Look, Ralph, what I'm going to be doing will have value only if you do your job well. Nothing else will count if that fails.'

It was logically true. And the reality of it must have sunk in, for Scudder said hastily, 'Don't worry. We can make a map for you, and we will.'

He pressed down on an intercom switch. 'Hey, Dan, come in here.'

It was a relief to feel the blindfold and to realize that he was finally going to be free again. He felt himself being guided to the door.

There was, at that instant, an interruption. It was a sound, muffled but with enormous shock in it, for the Shelters trembled.

And Marin, who had heard that sound before, in tests of weapons, in old films, felt a chill, then a flash of disbelief, then complete conviction. And then . . .

A loud-speaker broke into life somewhere near; and a strained voice said, 'Go to your nearest Shelter. An atomic bomb has just been exploded in the sector of Group 814, totally demolishing the Square. Go to your nearest Shelter and await further instructions. Repeat . . .'

CHAPTER TWENTY-THREE

Marin snatched the blindfold from his eyes and turned.

Scudder was hurrying to an inner room. At the door, he paused and looked back.

'Got to find where Group 814 is located. We may have to move some of our equipment – fast!'

Marin could have told him where. But he was thinking, 'Trask's apartment, Riva, his body . . .'

He stood, feeling numb yet calm. It seemed far away and unreal; not yet wholly true.

Near by, the loud-speaker sounded again, code words, which he recognized. Translated: 'All Group Masters report to Shelter Headquarters C.'

Marin stirred. 'Put the blindfold back,' he said. 'I have to get out of here before the Control bans air flight.'

It was a council of war, in the underground headquarters of the Great Judge.

Marin sat in a chair in front of an open door. Through this door came the official couriers of the armed forces, bringing him messages from the near-by emergency communications center which had been hastily activated by the military and which had taken over defense of the city from the special police force (under Slater) charged with its defense.

Some of the messages he handed to the Great Judge. These were usually extremely brief summaries of conditions on the surface. Streets were patrolled. A dozen looters had already been executed by firing squads. Trucks were moving emergency rations from outlying areas to the food stations in the Shelters, where, already, the task of feeding the millions at breakfast the following morning was under way. Most reassuring of all, the radioactive fall-out on the city was far below the danger point. Strong winds in the upper atmosphere had dispersed the deadly cloud.

Everywhere group leaders were coolly utilizing the many-leveled system of group responsibility to maintain order. Return to the city-above-ground would be carried on with selected elements of each group reoccupying residences and business establishments. Thus, each group would divide itself into four echelons, and only one echelon would be above ground at a time, until the emergency was over. Even if a second bomb exploded, without warning, the group would maintain itself.

It was presently clear to all those present that the danger of total catastrophe was already over. Men were relaxing. There were grim smiles of relief. Marin accepted several new messages, saw that they told the same story, sat back in his chair, and thought, What now?

The terrible error was forever made. In refusing to free Trask, earlier, he had condemned both Trask and himself to death. As Trask, unless he could somehow nullify the sentence, he would be executed soon. And Trask himself – the identity that was the real essence of Wade Trask – was already dead, instantly destroyed by the bomb, and destroyed along with it, or, rather, totally disintegrated, the body of David Marin.

It was several hours now since he had left Scudder's office. The memory of the initial shock remained, but the effect of the shock had faded. He was accustomed to thoughts of violence, and so he had suppressed the fear of this disaster and put his effort on all the things that had to be done.

Now his attention wandered from himself. The death of the body in the laboratory receded as a point of interest. He was irrevocably committed to being Wade Trask; and he did not doubt but that there would be action against Trask; the location of the explosion was too significant for Trask not to be considered in relation to it.

But in spite of the personal urgency, he found himself thinking of the purely military aspects of the bomb. He gazed at the destruction as shown on the huge television screen on one wall and he realized with excitement and interest that the experts would now have their day. What size atomic bomb could one of the famous squares contain?

He could see even through the shambles that the square had

proved itself. The shock wave had evidently bounced upward along each curving layer of that cunningly built square barrier. Upward, in and up on itself, and again upward, many times, perhaps, each time shattering into ever smaller segments what had already been destroyed. That was the theory of what would happen; and there it was in all its pulverized and repulverized desolation.

It remained to discover by analysis the size of the bomb that had thus been held in this militarily ideal explosion trap. And to discover how many people had been killed. So far ninety-four members of Group 814 were known to be alive. They had gone to other parts of the city after the group meeting, for entertainment, or to be with friends. They were being questioned by Slater's men. A report would be issued.

That train of thought ended for Marin as he saw that Medellin was talking to the Great Judge. As at a cue, both men glanced at Marin, and Medellin beckoned him.

Marin went over and bowed to the dictator. The great man inclined his head gravely in a courteous response. As Marin straightened, he had the flash thought of what Trask had said: that he would have to turn against the Great Judge, that he would have no recourse but to take over. Standing there, he couldn't imagine it. There was no reason for doing so that made sense to him. Here, in this remarkable leader, was the shaper of the group-free-enterprise state. Perhaps it wasn't a perfect state, but it was a compromise at such a height of achievement that no sane person would lightly act against it.

Marin thought gravely, He used his position to take Delindy from me. That could be a reason.

But he felt no fire of anger start. Because she would have had to agree. Perhaps she had agreed out of fear, but that was only perhaps. You didn't kill a man over a woman who was not resisting.

That left Wade Trask, condemned seditionist. Marin knew that no person had ever been more guilty of the crime than Trask. But, by a fantastic circumstance, he himself would pay the penalty of death. He could imagine killing the Great Judge to save his own life. But he could not imagine feeling justified in doing so.

And so, he wouldn't. Wouldn't kill. Wouldn't take over.

There had to be a reason other than personal safety. He had been too long connected with the army. Too many men had died doing their duty while following his orders for him, at this moment, to forget his oath and his honor.

There *had* to be a solution, although it did not lie in murder or usurpation. Yet it was unthinkable that he who was innocent should go down to death without first using every reasonable method of escape. It was too soon to think of such last resorts as confession – particularly since the Great Judge himself might be an unwitting agent of the Brain. . . . But, somehow, before the hour of execution, he must act.

He finished straightening up from his bow. And then, as the Great Judge nodded again, Marin looked at Medellin, who said, 'I have been authorized to offer you the congratulations of his excellency, the Great Judge, and of the council, on the efficient way in which your local command took full charge of this emergency.'

The formalness of the praise made Marin wonder if perhaps they were not on the air; and if perhaps this scene were not on view on all local and public television sets.

With that possibility in mind, he said, 'On behalf of the entire Capital command, I accept your congratulations.'

Actually, there had been no problem, nor had he anticipated difficulties. The armed forces were trained for emergencies in advance, and training was a matter of logic. One simply considered all possible circumstances that might arise, and then organized units, and indeed entire commands, to deal with them in a manner that included humanitarian as well as military necessities. Result was minimum friction with maximum accomplishment.

He realized that both Medellin and the dictator were relaxing. He presumed, still without turning to see, that, if they had been on the 'air', they were now off. Medellin's next words seemed to prove it, 'David!'

'Yes?'

'His excellency and I feel that the sooner the Jorgian war is won, the more certain we can be that incidents such as this do not recur.'

They were clearly guessing that the bomb had been exploded by desperate Jorgian spies. The enormous coincidence of its being Group 814 – and the association with Trask – had not yet been brought to their attention. And, of course, not knowing as he did what had happened in Trask's secret laboratory, they would not realize that only the Brain could be responsible for the bomb.

Medellin was speaking again. 'David, proceed with the attack as scheduled.'

'You may count on it, sir.'

'Leave the local situation to your deputy, and to the council.'

'Very well, sir,' said Marin.

He felt relieved, for he was now free of duties until take-off time.

Not that there was anything in particular he could do but wait. Events still had him in their grip, not he them.

Wait. . . .

CHAPTER TWENTY-FOUR

The massive rocket ship came down at about 6 A.M., at Camp A in the Urals, and streaked through the graying dawn brightness shimmering like some misty, silvery creation of metal and light.

As the colossal speed began to lessen, Delindy took her gaze from the TV screen which showed their landing as seen by the automatic cameras that metered their progress along the runway. She looked at him with slightly glazed eyes and a tense smile, and then evidently began to breathe again. For she gulped, and said, 'How fantastically wonderful? Do you do this often?'

Marin, who had made over two hundred rocket flights in eighteen years, shook his head. 'It's too dangerous!' he said, and smiled affectionately at her.

She reached up and stroked his cheek. She said, 'You're a modest person in an egotistical way, aren't you, dear?'

'It's only because I love you so much,' said Marin. And then, momentarily, he closed his eyes in astonishment, for he hadn't intended to say that, hadn't intended to come even near an emotional abyss. He leaned back and was aware of the woman watching him, and aware that she was also disturbed by his words.

'That sounded real,' she said softly. 'I didn't think it could be that real any more.'

'I didn't think so either,' said Marin. But he was more confident. He had crossed a bridge inside himself and was safe again on the hard ground of casual conversation. He changed the subject. 'I want you to stay pretty well in seclusion. Our bedroom is beautiful. You'll find it satisfactory for one or two days.'

Delindy said, 'You've told me all this before, dear. Remember?'

'Have I?' Marin was surprised momentarily. 'Yes, I guess I did. These maneuvers must really be on my mind.'

Maneuvers! he thought. He was still calling them that – particularly in speaking to Delindy. Actually, he had scarcely given them a thought. His mind was almost wholly absorbed with his own predicament. He kept mentally running into walls.

Later, as they climbed out of the car which had brought them to the official residence, and as they started along the walk, a young man who had been sitting in the garden alcove, evidently waiting, stood up and came forward. He was a big youth, and Marin recognized his son, David Burnley. He paused. For a moment he felt a desire not to have Delindy see this product of his loins. He had a father's critical feeling toward a child that has somehow missed living up to the family potentiality. His own father had been one of the great soldiers of the early war period. He himself was certainly not to be discounted. And now, here was his oldest child a below-par individual, or so it seemed.

The young man came up and said respectfully, 'Hello ... uh ... Dad.'

Marin nodded, and turned to Delindy. 'My dear, I want you to meet a young man whom I discovered just the other day. His mother sent me her token in the very first mating games ever held, and I was bold enough to dare to win her. It's an amazing thing to realize what time can do.'

Delindy held out her hand, smiled, and said, 'Any son of David Marin's is a friend of mine.'

Young Burnley was staring at her with a peculiar look on his face. And it was evident from his dazed expression that another male had fallen for that perfect face and body. 'Uh,' he said, 'I'm real happy . . . real happy to meet you.'

Marin rescued the boy from his obvious inability to deal with a mature and attractive woman. 'What have you been doing, David?'

'As you suggested, sir, I've been making a study of the royal family of Jorgia in all its ramifications, with the help of that Jorgian . . . uh . . . spy. When he discovered what we wanted the list for, he was very eager to help. And so we've got everything.'

'Good,' said Marin. 'Have it sent to my quarters. Or, better still, bring it yourself.'

Burnley was recovering from his shock state. 'I want to say . . . uh . . . Dad, that I appreciate the way you handled that affair. I realize you could have had him executed. Your mercy does you credit, sir, and I'm very proud to have your blood in me.'

Marin was amazed to realize that it was he, now, who was slightly embarrassed. He bowed, for want of any other response, took Delindy's arm, and started toward the door. Over his shoulder, he said, 'Be seeing you, David.'

Inside, he took out his handkerchief and wiped his brow, and said, 'I'm not really accustomed to talking to young people, as you probably observed.'

'You have to live with them from babyhood.' said Delindy calmly. 'My two youngsters are coming along, and I just take them in my stride.'

Marin was silent. The subject of Delindy's children had always disturbed him, in that he felt guilty at not having been there to see them. Both the children were his – which was unusual in that it was not considered genetically desirable to have the same life joined twice. Children of the same parents were too much alike. Such a union lacked randomness. But he had used his influence, and it emphasized once again the casual attitude of someone who considered himself above and beyond the group idea. Looking back, it seemed to Marin that his action then illustrated once again – if proof were needed – the insolence of power.

Delindy showed no sign of having a child by the Great Judge. Which was surprising, in view of that individual's known potency. Marin made a mental note to question her about it later.

Delindy was speaking again. 'Only one thing about the children worries me.'

'What's that?'

'The older has found out that you're the father of both of them.'

'So?'

She shook her head at him gently. 'My dear, it makes him different. He's ashamed. He's made me promise never to tell his friends.'

Marin pressed his lips, but he was not amused. This was the pressure of the new culture. Children were being offered new attitudes, and, like the little human sponges that they were, they were sopping it up.

People will fit any form, he thought, under pressure. Maybe that's what Trask meant. Their ability to conform has fooled all the observers.

Chameleons? Yes, but only for a while. Get the little creatures out under a hot sun. Forget that conformance was only a surface coloration. Keep things hot, and suddenly, one day, someone else would offer what looked like protective coloring, and they would make the switch. Never once would the individual himself be in view.

It was too big a thought to consider now. He said, 'My dear, I'm going to be busy most of the day. I'll come in when I can.'

Delindy came over and kissed him tenderly on the lips. 'I'll be here. What's on your agenda, principally?'

She spoke casually, but he noticed that she was ever so slightly tense. With any other suspect he would long ago have used a forcing method of getting information from her. But her position as the dictator's mistress made her untouchable. Nevertheless, as the daughter of a former Jorgian ambassador, Delindy had been kept in ignorance of the fact that this was to be an attack on the country of her birth. And he had his own reasons for believing that it was advisable not to give her any data which she did not already have.

He said, 'It will be important training maneuvers. I think you'll find them very — well, not boring. I'd like you to accompany me wherever possible.'

CHAPTER TWENTY-FIVE

At 8:00 A.M., he issued an order of the day that had been drawn up by Medellin, Slater, the Great Judge and himself during a long session two months before. It commanded that all active personnel would participate until further notice in a 'major operation.'

It called upon the 'good soldiers of this great force' to show 'your skill, daring and courage.' It stated that 'much depends' on the success of the important 'maneuvers which will now engage your attention' and 'mine' for many days to come. 'Outstanding achievements' by individuals would be 'immediately and gloriously rewarded by the Great Judge.'

The completed order resembled a dozen similar orders of the day of past years, yet it differed in its tone. The reader, or listener, could not escape the possibility that this was the long-awaited push.

In the Jorgian capital, where, of course, it would be sent by someone, its context would be anxiously scanned, and the question asked by the budget-minded ministers of the Queen would be: Should more troops be dispatched to defend the borders?

In their world of fantasy, they would imagine that a hundred thousand more unwilling men at the border would 'reinforce' the two hundred thousand who were already there.

Late in the day, word arrived that additional troops were being flown to the front by fleets of Jorgian planes.

Marin sighed when he heard the news. It would soon be evident who was fooling himself — he or the Jorgians. He was willing to wager that the methods used the past many years for determining the innermost thoughts of Jorgians had been scientific, and that therefore resistance would be small.

He joined Delindy about nine o'clock in the evening. He found her friendly, anxious to please him, but so tense that she could not respond to his advances. He surmised — without rancor — that here was a woman who was guessing that the country of her birth was about to be attacked. Outwardly she was unconcerned. But inwardly she was stricken with an intense anxiety. Perhaps, at some later time, when the conquest of Jorgia was history and the pain of her failure to prevent it only a memory, this woman would be able to be herself again.

It would be interesting to discover what she was like.

CHAPTER TWENTY-SIX

At 1:00 A.M., Camp A — actually vibrating with activity — was dimly lighted. In the half-darkness they were driven to the paraplane, which outwardly looked exactly like the other paratroop carriers. Inside, it was fitted out in the utmost luxury. There were a bedroom, an office, and a special room for an orderly and other crew members.

Marin and Delindy slept while the swift plane flew to a prearranged attack take-off point far to the south. And slept for more than two hours after the landing. A few minutes before four, Marin reached to the bedside table and turned off the alarm he had set. Since he had undressed only to the point of slipping off his shoes and his tunic, he now eased himself off the bed and went out into the office. He had barely finished dressing when a sound caused him to look up. It was Delindy. She came in and began to fix her hair as she said, 'I'd like to spend this time with you, if it's all right.'

Marin could not escape the thought that she was still the spy, working hard. He walked over to her, and they kissed.

She smiled at him — a tense smile. 'I'll stay out of your way.'

He wondered what she might still hope for. The situation seemed barren of opportunity. All orders were given. All troops were in motion. Nothing could now stop the attack. He went back to his desk and pressed a button.

The orderly room door opened, and a red-faced man of fifty entered and saluted. 'Bring me any messages that have arrived, Jennings.'

'Just one, sir. Just arrived. I haven't had time to type it from taking it down in longhand.' He laid a sheet of paper in front of Marin and went out.

It was a statement from the chief of staff. The armed forces had crossed the Jorgian frontier, and the war was on.

Marin read the coded message, and then glanced at Delindy. The time had come to tell her the truth. He did so quietly, and finished: 'You understand, I couldn't tell you sooner.'

She was pale but calm. She nodded, and said finally, 'Will you be in danger?'

Marin did not make a direct answer. He said instead, 'You don't seem disturbed.'

Delindy smiled wanly. 'I'm a little shaken,' she said. 'But everyone in Jorgia has been expecting this for years. We Jorgians have been engaged in mass self-delusion. We can only hope for understanding.'

'How do you mean?'

CHAPTER TWENTY-SEVEN

The woman had turned and was gazing through the transparent plastic wall. She seemed unaware of his gaze on her. She seemed different, somehow – a little harder, not so gentle. Perhaps that was something he had imagined her to have – the gentleness. It might actually never have been in her.

He thought, and he was more convinced now, She's either a Jorgian spy or unknowingly an agent of the Brain. She bore me two children to further her purposes as an agent, and then became the mistress of the dictator. And now she hopes for . . . understanding.

He said slowly, 'Suppose the Great Judge were to give me carte blanche as to what is to be done in Jorgia, what would you expect of me?'

Her answer went instantly beyond the limitations of his question. She did not face him, but she seemed suddenly breathless. She said, 'If you were the Great Judge, I would expect an alteration in the mating games permitting marriages after a certain age. I would expect that such states as

Jorgia would be granted considerable autonomy. I would expect a return of religious freedom. I would . . .'

Her voice went on, but it receded into the far background of his mind. *If you were the Great Judge . . .*

He thought, She would expect me to destroy the life work of the Great Judge and to substitute for it . . . weakness.

He had no feeling of condemnation; only a strange melancholy. He realized that she had stopped talking.

He said, 'Unfortunately – or perhaps fortunately – I'm not the Great Judge. But I will act for him for a few days in Jorgia.'

There was silence. Delindy walked out of his line of vision, behind him.

As he waited for her to respond to that, Marin noticed a paper on his desk, and its heading: *Summary of an Investigation into the Royal Family of Jorgia, by David Burnley.*

He picked up the document reluctantly, although he knew it might be valuable in guiding him in the snap decisions he would have to make on the morrow. Besides, he had brought it along out of curiosity. What quality of work had his son accomplished?

He glanced down the list of names – just over a hundred; and glanced at the supporting text, taking in the general meaning of whole paragraphs at one look. His attention focused abruptly on a sentence which read: 'The death of the Queen's younger sister, Andelindamina, a few years ago, reduced the direct line to the person of Queen Kijshnashenia herself.'

The next sentence was: 'The Queen is unmarried, and I have gathered that this was a deliberate policy to give the impression abroad that she might be the last of the line.'

Marin nodded, half to himself. He could guess the reason. If the Great Judge could be propagandized into believing that Jorgia would eventually fall without a struggle, then he might concentrate his military activity elsewhere. It was probably one of many delaying tactics that were meaningless now.

He put the paper down finally and realized that he had known most of what was in it before, though not in so sharp a form. The idea of policy in connection with the Queen's not marrying – that was new. And there were names and relationships that he had not connected. And such minor items as the name of the Queen's dead sister; he hadn't known that before.

His thought poised: *What* was her name again?

An*delind*amina!

He put the paper down and sat very still; and then he said, without looking around, 'Did you know the Queen's sister?'

There was a long pause. Then her voice came from behind him. 'Yes, I knew her.'

'What was she like?'

Again a pause. Then: 'Young and naïve. She died, you know.'

Marin guessed that was true, no matter how one looked at it. Physical death was more final, of course. But the transformation of a young innocent into a woman of the world could have something of death in it also.

If it were true – what he was thinking – then it had been cleverly done indeed. The daughter of the ambassador from Jorgia; the identification had slipped by the investigators. Not really surprising. States like Jorgia had only in recent years attempted to establish political bonds with the Great Judge.

And so the sister of the reigning queen had come, unsuspected, into the heart of the Judge's world, on a mission – which had now failed.

Sitting there, Marin had the distinct impression that here was someone who was in as extreme a state of shock as anything he himself had been in during the past few days. He pretended to be examining his son's report. But there was a mirror in front of and above him. And he could see her body in it from just below the shoulders down to just below her waist. She looked tense, and afraid.

Marin waited.

Her voice came finally, calm, casual: 'Who will you execute?'

So that was it.

Marin said, 'I'll determine that when I get there.'

He noticed that there seemed no doubt in her mind as to

the outcome of the battle. She accepted defeat for Jorgia without question.

'The Queen?' Delindy asked after a long pause.

'I have carte blanche!' said Marin deliberately.

There was a pause; then: 'She's a friend of mine.' She spoke in a small voice.

Marin sighed inwardly. He guessed that if his sudden insight were correct, he was listening to a woman appealing for the life of her sister.

It seemed to him that, although he could not reveal what had been planned for the Queen, he could offer a minimum reassurance to the sister. He said, 'If the matter, of –' he hesitated '– punishment comes up at all, I'll call you and discuss it with you, if you wish.'

'Thank you,' said Delindy. Her body seemed to relax, as he watched her in the mirror. 'I wish you would do that,' she said, and her voice was firmer.

Marin said, 'Consider it settled.'

He had only one personal, or near-personal, thought after that. For a few moments, the smoking desolation of the square of Group 814 floated up into his mind. The nightmarish picture, with all its deadly implications for him, and for the world of the Great Judge, lingered briefly. And then he turned his attention deliberately aside.

Less than an hour later he placed Delindy on a courier plane, which would take her back to Camp A. From there she would return by ordinary jet flight to the capital. And so on to a midwestern residence where she had already sent her children. She would remain there until the crisis in the capital was over.

CHAPTER TWENTY-EIGHT

By nine o'clock the early morning mist had dissipated. Below his plane, the mountains made a bright, green picture in the brilliant sunlight. Through the transparent bottom of the loaded paratroop carrier, Marin could see here and there the beginning of farmland.

Several towns flashed by below, and then a glitter of movement below, in the near sky – attack planes shooting up at the carrier formations. They were intercepted somehow, because he did not see that group again.

At 9:30, his heart beating just a little faster, Marin jumped and came down successfully within a quarter of a mile of a predetermined landing range.

Near by, magnetic-powered jets discharged by giant carriers began to land and disgorge an array of glittering mechanical devices. Within minutes tanks, mobile guns, and transport vehicles were whipping around, picking up personnel.

At about 10:30, a paratroop army, paced by barriers of mobile metal – ready to spit death against all resistance – was converging from every point of the compass along all the main through streets and the important side streets of a city that seemed deserted, except for frightened faces peering out of windows.

Marin saw no fighting. He arrived at the palace shortly before noon with an armored escort and found it already being patrolled by his own men.

Inside, the special guards he had assigned leaped to attention at their officer's command as he entered. The captain came over and saluted. He said in a low voice, 'The Queen is in the throne room, and we're just getting our lab people into position for when you enter to talk to her.'

Marin nodded. What was about to happen had been carefully planned. He said, 'As soon as everything is in readiness, have a chamberlain announce me.'

It was only a few minutes later that he entered the room, which was actually a receiving chamber for formal occasions when not too many guests were involved. The Queen herself sat stiffly in a tall-backed chair. She was a young woman, very plainly made up, her hair braided, her face without cosmetic care – but he would have recognized her immediately as being related to Delindy. It was not a strong resemblance. The Queen very definitely did not have the classic beauty of her sister. But in the line of the nose and the jaw, in the curve of the cheek, and, subtly, in the shape of the head, the Queen and Delindy were unmistakably similar. She was dressed now in a drab, brown, silklike gown, which seemed to come down to just below her knees.

Marin started forward and then paused to bow. The woman inclined her head. As he straightened, Marin saw that a technician was entering the room through a door which was to one side and slightly behind the Queen.

Without glancing at Marin, the man pointed his gas pistol and fired at the woman. As she slumped over, the mobile unit rolled in behind the technician. Marin remained where he was and watched two women lift the Queen and lay her face down on the padded rest under the circuit projector.

The machine purred, and although nothing was visible, at that instant the fateful circuit was impressed on her shoulder muscles. Henceforth, and for the rest of her life, a sub-unit of Control Center could be activated and could start a pain of gradually increasing intensity in the shoulder area.

And still Marin did not move. As he watched, the women lifted the Queen from her prostrate position and placed her in the chair in which she had been sitting. The mobile unit began to withdraw. It went out of the door through which it had come and presently only the technician remained. Marin nodded to him, and he fired a second gas gun at the woman in the throne chair. Then he withdrew.

She stirred, and opened her eyes, and saw Marin. Marin said, 'I beg your pardon, your majesty, I'll send your women in to you and call on you this evening.'

She was shaking her head, as if trying to clear her mind of mists. She murmured, 'I don't seem to ... I don't know what ...' She spoke an almost accentless English.

'I'll send your ladies,' said Marin.

He bowed, turned on his heel, and walked out. In the anteroom, he spoke to the chief of guards, and then he hurried to the new attack headquarters, which had now been set up in the principal military establishment of the captured Jorgian capital.

The building pulsed with hurrying men. For a time, messages from the interior were sporadic. About three in the afternoon, however, as Marin ate a sandwich and drank a cup of coffee, he was handed a sheaf of messages. A hasty glance through them indicated the completeness of the victory. Organized resistance had virtually ceased, and nowhere had there been serious fighting.

He returned the papers for staff appraisal and rapid précis work, and then lay down for an hour. At that time, staff work and additional reports established that the 'great' Jorgian war was over.

He turned his attention to reports of interviews with government leaders. All denied any connection with the bomb that had exploded in the square of Group 814. Lie detectors verified their statements.

Questions pertaining to knowledge of some secret group working out of Jorgia brought forth less positive data. Answers like: 'There were, and are, so many experimental groups'; 'I know of none that would resemble obsolete Communism'; 'Idealists – we have them in great herds.'

For Marin, these answers simply established that the Jorgian government was not involved. He detached special units of military intelligence to watch all border posts, particularly those leading to two states not under the control of the Great Judge.

'On 9/1 to 9/3,' he wrote, 'arrest and hold all persons attempting to leave Jorgia. Give lie detector tests to every person, man or woman, who seems to be either an idealist type or of unusual intelligence.'

He had to admit to the colonel in charge of Intelligence that that was a vague directive. Could a person who was still plotting Communism be considered intelligent? 'Let's say, Rex,' he said sardonically to the officer, as he ended the interview, 'that the appearance of intelligence may be there, but it will show selective blind spots.'

He next instructed his field secretarial chief. 'Have all reports on the bomb interviews tele-transmitted to the Great Judge.'

He himself sent the dictator a formal message.

'Your excellency, the police forces, which you so generously authorized to be placed at the disposition of Her Majesty of Jorgia, Queen Kijshnashenia, have fulfilled the purpose for which they were loaned. At the request of her majesty, our forces are being used for guard purposes in outlying areas, but it is expected that loyal Jorgian troops will be able to take over full responsibility within a week. All over outbreaks of revolution have been quelled. The lawful government of Jorgia is again functioning.'

He signed it 'David Marin, Group Master.'

Late in the afternoon, Slater arrived, glowing with a kind of poisonous glee. The two men had dinner in an atmosphere of relative peace, broken by the faint sound of occasional gunfire. For a while they talked of the war. Then Marin – who was more interested than he wanted to indicate – asked if anything more had been learned about the bomb. Slater shook his head. He seemed impatient, and so Marin let the matter drop.

Over coffee, they discussed a list of names of men who had been marked for assassination but who, for one reason or another, had been made prisoner instead. There were eighty-two individuals involved, and they did a very simple thing: each took a copy of the list and checked off the names of men whom they still believed should be executed. Marin marked only eight names; Slater, as it turned out, checked off thirty-one.

They compared the marked names on their respective lists and found that seven of Marin's people were also on Slater's.

At that point Slater picked up a phone and called the prison where the men were being held. He read off the seven names and finished curtly: 'Destroy them immediately.' He hung up and turned back to Marin. 'Now, let's decide about these others.'

Marin nodded. He was a little amazed that he had no feeling about the matter. The death that threatened him seemed to have no relation to his present situation. The thought did cross his mind that all these individuals had their own survival to attend to. If they could do it, fine; if they couldn't, too bad.

His job required that he examine their potential as dangerous persons during the next year, on the basis of their careers. A single false evaluation, and not one but a thousand individuals might die.

He had his son's list brought in and compared the hundred and ten names on it with the names Slater had marked for death. Eighteen of them were the same.

Marin shook his head at the little man and smiled. 'The Queen's relatives,' he said. 'Not to be killed as yet.'

It reminded him, and he glanced at his watch. After nine. 'We'll have to leave this,' he said. 'You know what I'm supposed to do to that woman. It's time I was doing it.'

Slater stood up restlessly. 'I have to be going also,' he said. 'A lot of decisions to make on the spot.' He warned: 'We'll have to decide on these men in the morning, though. One more thing, before you go.'

'Yes?'

'Did you find anything on the Brain?'

'No.'

'Thank you. Good luck with the Queen.'

Marin smiled and said the bantering words that were expected of a male: 'It's at times like this when I really appreciate being a Group Master.'

CHAPTER TWENTY-NINE

He arrived at the palace a little before ten and went directly to the Queen's personal apartment. As he entered, the woman, who had been sitting in a chair, jumped to her feet and faced him.

Her eyes were widened beyond what seemed normal. She looked fatigued, and there was a stiffness about her that denoted a measure of fear. Her voice, when she spoke, was an attempt at calm, but the attempt was only partially successful.

She said, 'You're going to kill me, aren't you? The Great Judge always orders the death of the leaders of the territory he takes over. I want you to know that I am ready for death, but wish to make one request of my conqueror.'

It was not the moment to disillusion her about her fate. But there was no doubt that she was in a melodramatic state. He guessed he was about to have some sort of emotional appeal made to him. He said, in an even voice, 'Any reasonable request, which does not conflict with my instructions, will be granted to your highness.'

She came toward him, swaying a little, and there was a hint of imminent tears in the way she held her mouth, and in her voice, as she said, 'General, to you this conquest of Jorgia may only be an episode, but for me it is the end of an era. In my death throes, I have wild thoughts about many things. To me, being the conquered is laden with symbolic meanings, and somehow the conqueror is interwoven into these symbols. I am woman, conquered, and you are man, conqueror. Although I had no more than a fleeting glimpse of you . . . earlier . . . I had then the feeling of fear and hate . . . and love.'

He didn't have to lock the door. That had been done automatically on his earlier instructions.

He lifted the woman lightly into his arms and carried her into the bedroom. The fire that was in her made her reach for him. She had strength, this woman, at this moment, as she grasped at him and pulled him down.

In the pale light of dawn, they lay side by side, exhausted but not asleep, and she said, 'You'll never forget me, will you?'

'Never,' said Marin.

'You may kill me now,' she said, sighing. 'I feel a rightness in me. The defeat is consummated.'

And he thought, wonderingly, Perhaps it had been *two* condemned people clutching at a last fling of life. For, unless he could find a solution to his problem, he was really condemned. And she thought she was.

He stirred, in a thoughtful way, and realized what he had forgotten during those moments of passion – that the time had come to offer life to her. He felt the change to thought level function within himself, the transition from simple cell-man to complex being. He said, 'Shenia, I've been thinking. Maybe there is a way. Maybe we can figure a way for your family to remain in control. I might be able to justify an expedient solution.'

'My whole family?' she said, surprised. 'You mean, relatives?'

'Why not?' said Marin. 'A hundred are as easy as one.'

'But wouldn't that be dangerous for you?'

Marin said carefully, 'I didn't say I could do it. I said maybe we can think of a way. You'd have to agree to things you've never agreed to before.'

'You'll do those things, anyway,' she said, intent. 'If I could save my family . . .' She paused. 'Why are you doing this?' she asked wonderingly, her tone of voice almost like that of a child. And then, before he could speak, she asked another question: 'For me?'

'For you!' said Marin.

That was all. She seemed to accept that. Nor was it unusual. The plan had been that she would henceforth feel that she had a protector in the top echelon of the Great Judge's councilors. The fact that this particular councilor was, unknown to everyone, scheduled for death did not affect the validity of the idea for this moment.

Lacking the decisive communication the two of them had achieved, she might have been obstinate – or dramatized her defeat in a die-for-my-people gesture. As it was, she signed the documents he presented to her and made a combined network radio-TV speech confirming that 'a fantastic revolution by elements whose goals were insane in view of the world situation has made it necessary for me to ask the protection of the Great Judge for myself and for my people.'

In the brief announcement, she pointed out sadly that 'acceptance of aid will necessitate certain changes, but the changes are preferable to uncontrolled bloodshed.' She finished by stating: 'To facilitate emergency action, I have accepted the resignation of Kugarachar Mayett and have asked Duoni Havariste to form a cabinet. . . .'

Local names, local people and time-honored methods – all utilized now in a lightning war, the full story of which would possibly never be known to the people of Jorgia or by the great mass of people anywhere. Slater was moving in with his teams of 'registrars.' A hundred thousand individuals, known for their adherence to monarchistic principles and marked for years as dangerous on a lower rating, had top priority for 'registration.' The process would be undignified when accomplished in such mass action. Proud men and women would have their self-esteem injured as they stood in long lines before the mobile units. Each individual would be fingerprinted, would sign his name to an affidavit, and would then lie face-down under a massive electronic device, usually identified as an X-ray photographic unit. Actually, it was the machine that impressed on the shoulder muscles of each person the circuit which could thereafter be activated to start a gradually increasing pain.

They could not relax until that job was completed, Marin knew. But he did not wait. Shortly before noon he called Medellin.

CHAPTER THIRTY

'My friend, I leave you your domain.'

Medellin was grave. 'You have my best wishes, David. An all-round brilliant performance, a personal triumph. Be sure to visit the Queen at least once a year, to re-establish your friendship.'

'You can have your secretary remind me,' said Marin dryly.

But inwardly, briefly, he recalled the excitement of the night. And knew that, if he had a future, he would seek again and again to recapture the experience.

Perhaps it had all started out as a scheme on the woman's part to save her life. But if it were, the Queen had won her victory out of the press of her own life stuff. He did not doubt but that there would be a child. It may indeed have been a scheme to seduce him. But it was a seduction that embraced the total being of the seducer.

Her plan or her need, whichever it was, had promoted his own purposes. She would be free to call on him – if he were alive. As a protector, he would, of course, normally provide her with any aid she desired – after discussion.

Medellin was speaking. 'I'll see you in a few weeks,' he said.

Marin said good-by, hung up, and flew back to Camp A. En route, his plane's escort fought off a lone Jorgian ship, which went tumbling down in flames. Marin soberly considered the motivations of the pilot's insane gesture, recalled Queen Kijshnashenia's intensely emotional dramatization of imminent death, and wondered what gestures he would make as the hour of midnight of the seventh day approached.

While waiting for his rocket at Camp A, he granted an interview to David Burnley and found that young man in a buoyant state of mind.

'Great work, Dad,' he said warmly. 'The way you handled it,

thousands of lives were saved — and, of course, it had to be done. I only wish I'd had a bigger part in it.'

Marin told him of the eighteen men whose names had been struck off the execution rolls as a result of being on the list prepared by young Burnley.

The effect of that was startling. Tears came into his son's eyes. Silently, the young man shook his hand. Afterward — after the interview was over — Marin thought, What kind of future will we have, with an entire generation of over-emotional young people just now coming of age? He visualized future groups filled with adults who had been virtually fatherless in their childhood and youth — tearful people by the million influencing the pattern of group law on the basis of their own inner need for the missing male parent.

Was that a true picture? he wondered. If it were, it did not augur well for the future of the land.

While he waited for take-off time, he found himself uneasy and unhappy. The fact was he didn't know what had been happening during his absence. They would unquestionably have turned on the pain circuit, the moment they discovered the connection between Trask and Group 814. The area covered would gradually be extended; better get drugs he could take when the rocket ship landed.

He'd stand the pain until his arrival. He didn't wish to appear doped before the officers who would meet him.

As it turned out, the ship was already past the apex of its climb when, abruptly, he felt the stab of pain through his shoulder.

As he silently fought the agony, one thing was clear to Marin: the crisis had arrived.

CHAPTER THIRTY-ONE

Marin twisted uneasily in his seat as the pain edged through his attempt to turn his attention wholly away from it. On the television screen in front of him, he saw that the machine was slanting sharply toward earth; and he could feel the deceleration in his stomach. The landing was precise and, as usual, routine in a dramatic fashion. When it had come to a stop, and the door was open, he slipped the first pill into his mouth. Then he stood up and walked a little stiffly down to the ground. There he stopped.

People were waiting for him, a reception committee, a delegation. Marin had expected officials from his own department. But now he saw that it was a famous reception committee indeed that waited for him: Podrage, half a dozen of the Group Masters and, standing off to one side, the Great Judge.

The recognition shocked him. He visualized many hours going by before he could get full relief from his pain. His thought reached that point, and then the dictator strode over, and his powerful hands gripped Marin's shoulders. 'David!' the leader shouted above the roar of the machines. 'Medellin tells me the job in Jorgia is done.'

Marin yelled back, 'Your excellency, Jorgia collapsed like a house of cards. It was a five-hour war.'

The great man hugged him gleefully. 'Good old David, still the greatest architect of lightning war in the history of the world.'

The remark startled Marin. He had never heard such unqualified admiration expressed before, nor had he thought of himself as anything but a sound concept logician functioning well in a special field.

Still chuckling, the Great Judge pulled him toward the other men. 'Oscar,' he said to Podrage, 'shake hands with a man who can't lose.'

Marin felt those narrow, steely eyes studying him; and then this most capable of all the Group Masters was shaking his hand. Podrage indicated the leader affectionately. 'This is a great occasion for the boss. With the fall of Jorgia, the world he dreamed of more than twenty years ago becomes real. There's nothing left big enough to be troublesome.'

That was not literally so. There could be a few dangerous coalitions. But it was true enough. Marin managed a tense smile. 'Oscar, Jorgia ought to keep us busy for a while, crunching, digesting.'

His startlement had yielded to uneasiness. He recalled once before when he had heard the Great Judge overpraise someone. Within hours, the man had been dead.

Marin thought shakily, I've got to remember that he began to have doubts about me over Trask. The question was: Could this strange ruler ever regain his confidence in any man once he had lost it?

Presently, the handshaking was over. The Great Judge's firm fingers gripped Marin's arm. 'Gentlemen,' he said to the group, 'the problem that remains is so important that I want us to go right now to where the bomb was exploded. I want David brought up to date, and the best place is right on the scene.'

They walked in a body to a large hopjet and were soon in the air, with an array of escort vessels flying before and behind. Marin's first glimpse of the devastated area was of searchlights blazing far ahead. As they drew near, he saw that the lights had been set up on every building that was still standing, and that the area swarmed with workers and equipment.

Even as he watched, he listened to Podrage, to the dictator himself and to an aide in his own department. And so, by the time they landed, he had a summary of what had happened in the time since the explosion. An additional eight members of Group 814 had been discovered as having left the city immediately after the meeting. This brought the total of survivors of the group to one hundred and two. And that seemed to be the total list; for no individual had come forward in the past twenty-four hours.

Podrage said, 'When we discovered that 814 was the group of Wade Trask, we had a feeling that a new dimension had been added to the cause side of this affair. We turned the pain circuit on a short time ago and so we should know soon if he's alive. I can't imagine what he would gain by an explosion, but its being his group is too big a coincidence. It must mean something.'

Marin, tense with pain, had the impulse to say, 'Maybe he was the target.' With an effort, he restrained the impulse and said instead, 'Suppose he doesn't appear?'

'Then that closes another door.'

Marin nodded. He hadn't really needed anyone to tell him something so obvious. But his mind kept drifting ever so slightly into areas of pain haze, and that took the edge off his alertness. . . . 'There is,' said the aide's voice beside him, 'evidence that the bomb was dropped from the air. However, the chart of flight graphs over the area indicates that the machine which

125

carried the bomb ended its journey by diving into the blast.'

A pilotless plane! Its entire flight over the city would be recorded on the automatic flight graphs. If it came from beyond the city limits, there would be radar charts of its flight going back across the continent.

'The plane,' said the aide's voice, 'took off from Parking Area B, in the center of the city. According to the records of Parking Area B, this ship had landed precisely five hours and ten minutes earlier at one of the freight outlets. Flight graphs of its landing indicate that it flew over the city from the east. The radar record takes it back to the Atlantic Coast, and from there long-range radar projectors have traced its origin to a submarine lying about two hundred miles offshore. Within a minute after the bomb blast the submarine blew up, sending a shock wave which was recorded by all the marine stations along the Atlantic. The timing of these recordings has enabled us to locate the exact position of the explosion. We know, therefore, that the submarine sank in water nearly one and three quarter miles deep. Exploration with instruments indicates that segments of metal are lying on the bottom at that location. When various neutrals were apprised of this information, they immediately denied that any of their submarines were missing. No further data.'

The aide was, for a moment, the only person whose attention was on Marin. Marin leaned toward him. 'Check on the disposition of all submarines built during the last fifty years.' He spoke in a low voice. 'Report to me personally.'

'Yes, sir!' said the man.

Marin leaned back. Not for the first time he realized how difficult it had been for anyone to set off an explosion in the Judge's City. His guess was that it was a bomb from long ago and far away indeed. He had a vague recollection that much equipment, including submarines, had disappeared in the maelstrom of war more than a quarter of a century before. He visualized agents of the Brain removing such equipment to innumerable hiding places, converting each unit so that it could be remote-controlled – and so, a submarine had emerged from its secret chamber, launched a robot plane, and had then waited until its instruments registered the explosion, at which time it had blown up.

He saw that they were coming down now. He quickly scanned the area of destruction and saw that much cleaning up had been done. He leaned toward his aide and said, 'How soon did the radioactivity clear up?'

The man answered, 'The explosive material was one of the very heavy elements, created the instant before blast, with a half-life of one one-hundredth of a second. Within minutes after the explosion, radioactivity was already well below danger point.'

Marin nodded, and his mind was very active again. He said, 'About ten years ago Major-General Inskip retired. Is he still alive?'

'Yes, he is. Over eighty, but strong.'

Marin said slowly, 'He was the greatest authority on weapons of the last century that I ever talked to – and they really had weapons in the second atomic war. I want you to send a commission of weapons experts over to see him and get the information I know he's been compiling. I'm specifically interested in what defenses were used against the various assault methods.'

His aide said, 'I'm sure Inskip will be delighted to see us. I hear he's been feeling neglected.'

Marin's attention was on the explosion again. 'So the bomb material had a very brief half-life,' he said thoughtfully.

Podrage, who had turned and had been listening, said, 'Whoever directed the bomb evidently had the minimum goal of destroying that one square and whoever was in it, but nothing else. Even before your message that you could find no evidence of a Jorgian bomb conspiracy, we had the feeling that they were not involved.'

Marin said, 'What did you discover at the freight station where the plane with the bomb landed?'

It was the aide who replied. 'That drew a blank. The machine merely used the area as a parking place, and neither loaded nor unloaded equipment.'

'I see,' said Marin. 'It waited there for instructions, or else it was geared to a timing device.'

What shocked him was that so much valuable material had been sacrificed, and so many risks taken, to destroy one aspect of human activity about which the Brain felt uncertain. He did not question the great thinking machine's reasoning. Its estimate of the extent of the danger was exactly right. But the fact that it had reacted so remorselessly sharpened his awareness of the value of Trask's invention.

He wondered uneasily, Can a man in possession of such an instrument let himself be defeated by default?

A little later, as he stood amid the desolation of what had been Trask's apartment, the feeling of uneasiness was a pulsing rhythm with the pain that kept groping through to him. Most of the floor was relatively intact. Markers indicated the relativeness with such words as *Safe* or *Doubtful* or *Dangerous* or – in several places – *Acutely Dangerous*. Marin avoided the latter, but he walked without hesitation into what had been the bedroom, one side of which was labeled *Dangerous*. There was no sign of the beds or of the body. He asked about that casually, and the guide looked down a list he carried in one hand, and said, 'No bodies found on this entire floor, sir.'

Over and above the nagging pain, Marin had a reaction to that. It was as if he had somehow been hoping all this time, and now, suddenly, there was no hope. He felt the letdown, a kind of apathy of acceptance, a dull conviction that the worst was true, and a great sadness. He looked toward where he remembered having seen Riva that first night, her nude, tanned body half covered by the sheets of the bed. And then he visualized the same body at the instant of the titanic explosion, charred and smoldering, quickly burned to a fine ash. And in the shattered buildings all around him the members of Group 814, who had offered Wade Trask their good will, had died in a flash of dissolving fire. What was immensely disturbing was that they had died because he had discovered a secret.

As he walked stiffly over the broken floor, back to where the laboratory had been, he had another thought: Even if he could survive the sentence of death, the Brain would search ceaselessly for the individual – himself – who knew of its existence. And, accordingly, it was time to be logical.

'Am I going to try to save myself?' Marin asked himself the question.

He had been waiting, he realized tensely, for something to happen that would automatically get him out of his predicament. He thought, Suppose I handled this entire affair as if it were a military campaign – who is the enemy?

The Brain?

He felt restless and indecisive. He bent down painfully and pushed a charred metal bar out of the way. And then he was able to look at the spot where – if his calculation was correct – his own body had lain. Right here, two days ago, the awareness entity that was Wade Trask inhabiting the body of David Marin had met instant death. Because of that event, the issue was now confused, but not too much. If the enemy were truly the Brain, then he could treat everyone else as if they were but puppets.

'They were . . .' He tried to think it with intense conviction. 'They *are*!'

How could any competent authority fail to find the Brain? All those who were looking must be agents of the Brain. The entire search for such a massive structure was a farce. It was impossible to fail. He recalled Slater's words and attitude, the secrecy of the search. Every Control officer who sought with such apparent determination was sworn to silence, and somehow they had managed to create a mental attitude whereby it became dangerous for anyone to remember that the Brain existed.

Marin walked to where the clock had been, and again bent down – this time to see if any exposed connections were visible. But inwardly he was looking at the picture of the Brain that he had conceived. And the only problem was: Where was it hiding? The best possibility was still the Shelters below the Great Judge's residence – the safest place on all this planet. But safe only if the Great Judge was an agent of the Brain.

Marin straightened up, wincing a little as he did so. But he was visualizing key men in the human race controlled by a thinking machine. Looking back on it now, he could see that the machine had had an almost insoluble problem, the problem of securing its own safety. Its solution had been brutal almost beyond imagination. Using its two principal agents – the Great Judge and Slater – the Brain had destroyed every person who had actively helped it conceal itself, and simultaneously it had convinced its agents that they were committing mass murders because of a sincere determination to destroy the Brain. It was conviction on the impact level. As murder followed murder, all doubt must have been suppressed in them as to their own motives. But the fact was, only the Brain had gained from the prolonged, futile search.

Marin grew aware that the Great Judge was standing beside him. The dictator said, 'What is it, David?'

Marin pointed to the perforations in the mental beam, which must have held the wiring of the clock. 'I was wondering what that was, your excellency.'

'Call the guides. They have complete maps and plans.'

The plans showed no such perforations had been authorized for the building. Accordingly, a notation was made. It meant that every worker who had ever signed in on any repair contract for the building would be questioned with a lie detector. That would require several days, even a week, Marin estimated.

He was not actually concerned. He had seen for himself that nothing remained of Trask's apartment. It was not enough to have guessed the reality of that from an image on a television screen. In a peculiar way, he had needed to come here to the scene, and look at the destruction, and feel the rubble with his feet, and smell the aftermath of the bomb.

He felt abruptly weary. He was a man who had now established that his own body was no longer in existence. Even if nothing else ever threatened him, there would still be the fact that he didn't want Trask's body as replacement. Suppose that somehow he got out of immediate danger. Would he then 'settle down' in Trask's body? The prospect made him gloomy. At best, it would be a life of continuous disguise.

He thought, what I need right now is four hours of drugged sleep, free of pain. And then I can get going.

A hand touched his arm. Marin turned and saw that it was an officer of the Great Judge's personal guard – a Pripp. Four other Pripp officers were walking toward him. They looked oddly alert.

The first Pripp said in a formal tone, 'I have instructions from his excellency, the Great Judge, to place you under arrest. I advise you to come quietly.'

Marin said, in dismayed anger, 'You have *what*?'

'You are under arrest, sir.'

Marin turned his back on the officer. The weight of disaster was already heavy on him, and he had little doubt but that here was the fruition of his uneasy feelings over the Great Judge's actions. He saw the dictator standing off to one side, with Podrage and two other Group Masters. They were all watching him.

'Your excellency,' Marin called, 'I don't understand this.'

The heavy face was cool, insolent, self-possessed. '*Mister* Trask,' said the Great Judge, 'there are many things that we don't understand either. One of these things is: What has happened to our dearly beloved David Marin?'

Marin parted his lips to speak, and then he closed them again. He shook his head ever so slightly, as if he would clear from his mind the fog of pain that was settling over him. And then he thought that his earlier hunch had been right, though in a different way, and that here, before he was ready, was the crisis. The Great Judge spoke again, in a grim voice, 'You will, I assure you, have a full opportunity to explain yourself, prior to your execution.'

He broke off curtly. 'Take him to the Control prison.'

CHAPTER THIRTY-TWO

They took no chances. He was handcuffed before he was led aboard a special Control plane. Once aboard, he was subjected to a search, which was polite. But he would have considered it thorough, preliminary to disguise removal, had he been in charge of the group who did it.

The search included examination of his teeth – Marin was astonished when it actually produced a hollow false tooth, with some kind of chemical in it. The search did not include examination for insertions of capsules into muscles, nor was there any examination of his skin to see if sections had been painted with certain dyes – soluble in water as drugs. The search did include scraping his fingernails clean, and ended with all his clothes being exchanged for a simple light coverall coat and trouser combination, gray in color. All this before the hopjet landed at the top of the Group Masters' building. He was led, manacled, to a concrete and steel prison, which was a part of Slater's department.

There, special agents removed the Marin disguise. In half an hour Marin was identified by photographs and Control records as the condemned seditionist, Wade Trask.

It was grimly interesting to Marin to notice the change in the demeanor of his captors as the disguise came off, one circuit at a time. They became rougher. Whereas they had been considerate while the resemblance to Marin remained, now the hands that touched him shoved, and squeezed, and pinched, and gripped, always faster, tighter, or harder than was necessary. Finally, one of the bigger men stepped forward, grabbed his shoulders, and, instead of requesting him to sit down, tried to impel him forcibly back into a chair.

Marin upthrust his knee into the other's groin and heard the moan as the man reeled backward, fell to the floor and lay there, writhing. From Marin's right, a second man struck him on the side of the head. But he had expected blows; and for many minutes he had been generating the hatred and rage that alone could enable a human being to withstand torture. And so the fist striking him was merely a vague numbness. It shattered again the emotional barrier of his anger.

With that thick film of hatred as a protection, he kicked the shins of the individual who had struck him. And then – since he still had all his wits about him – he sat down in the chair before there could be any further reaction. He knew from his own experience that it was psychologically easier to strike a man who was standing than one who was sitting.

From the back of the room, an authoritative voice said, 'Leave him alone. We're supposed to await orders on him.'

The big man picked himself up off the floor and limped over to a cot and sat down. The other agent let go of his ankle and walked with visible painfulness over to a chair and sank into it.

At this point, Marin was able to observe that there were six men in the room. All had the look of being Control officers; two were men in their early thirties and looked young and capable. Three were big men, in their forties. The leader was gray-haired and perhaps fifty-five.

He came forward. 'Mr. Trask,' he said. 'My name is Martin Carroll. I expect shortly to receive orders to obtain from you, by any means, a full account of your activities.'

Marin studied the man's face. He was remembering Carroll. He had seen him once or twice with Slater, he recalled. Carroll was a type. Strongly dedicated to duty, he was a dangerous adversary because he had no doubt about the rightness of the work he did.

Marin had only a passing interest in the man. He knew his own needs in what was developing here. Only hate in all its violence could maintain the muscles and nerves of any living creature against torture. He had no time for kind thoughts or for reason – except at the far edge of his mind.

There was a sound at the door. Carroll walked over and spoke for several minutes to someone Marin couldn't see. Then the door shut, and Carroll came back. He stopped, and placed himself squarely in front of Marin. 'The orders have arrived,' he said. His voice was calm, but some of the color had gone out of his cheeks. 'As soon as you're ready to talk, let me know, and I'll call the Great Judge. He wants to hear this himself.'

CHAPTER THIRTY-THREE

Marin had no awareness of how much time went by, then. Whenever he felt pain, he raised his voice in paroxysms of rage and hate. He knew only vaguely what he said. Much of it was taunting of his tormentors, unintelligible and unintelligent. The words didn't matter. The emotion, and any and every reason for maintaining it – that alone counted.

The basic reason for not speaking was unutterably real. He could not, must not, dare not, tell his story to men who were controlled by the Brain. . . . Until all other possibilities were exhausted.

He had a feeling, out of his own experience, that they would not kill him until they had learned something from him. And so, to tell was to die, and not to tell was to live.

There was no time, and all time, under the glare of lights in this inner chamber. He was a man who maintained life in his body by feeding on the raw stuff of his nerves. Again and again he drained his strength and came down to the depth of exhaustion, only to find a new reservoir of hate, which seemed to flood his whole being with a fire of renewed energy.

At such moments he almost literally vibrated physically with the violence of his feeling. He shouted, in a high, intense voice, one negation after another: 'Idiots – fools – slaves – stupid, stupid, stupid . . .' over and over again.

At no time did he feel any pity for himself, nor did it occur to him to ask for mercy, nor did he have any sense of being genuinely critical of what they were doing. Rightness or wrongness was not at issue. He had seen men in all stages of physical, moral and mental disintegration, and only those who held onto a kind of insane rage survived at all. That was the fact, the single, important fact.

His sustained rage began to affect his interrogators – as he had known it would – although he had no plan about it. The very inner violence which had drawn each of these men into Control work was an unsuspected weakness, stimulated now. The barriers of outward calmness went down, one by one, before that most dramatic of all emotions.

And, suddenly, a man was screaming. And they carried him out, kicking and fighting, like a little boy in a tantrum; only he was a big boy, and it took all the strength of several Control officers to hold him.

A second man began to sob quietly; and Carroll went over to him and said, 'Dan, you're ruining your reputation. Stop it!'

'I can't help it,' the man said, sobbing. And they took him out.

There was one other among that shaken group. He froze, a rigid state, all the muscles locked, eyes staring. A doctor hastily gave him a shot in the arm, and he fell over limply, like a rag doll.

Somewhere in there Carroll must have notified the Great Judge. Because, all at once, the door opened, and through a gray haze Marin saw that the dictator had arrived. He stood just inside the doorway, a large, puzzled man; and he shook his leonine head, and he said, 'Stop the procedure. Let him rest. Take him to . . .'

Marin didn't hear where he was to be taken. He had slumped over. Even as he felt hands grip him, he fell into a sleep that was dangerously close to unconsciousness.

Marin yawned. Then he opened his eyes. Then he remembered. He was sitting in a chair, in a large, tastefully furnished room. His wrists were manacled to the arms of the chair. And there was a numbness in his lower limbs that resolved presently into awareness that his ankles were manacled to the legs of the chair.

His head was free to move, so he glanced around, hoping for some view that would identify where he was. A closed door to his right, a wall television, no windows, a settee to his left, a large clock in the wall in front of him, and . . .

His attention poised, and he thought, sickened, It's a clock like Trask's.

As he glared at it, it *brred* softly and struck the half hour: ten-thirty – whether morning or night, he had no idea. The sound had died away when a silvery bright streamer flowed to the floor from a hidden orifice of the clock. It wriggled there and coiled like a rope, as the clock continued to manufacture more of the substance.

Abruptly, the coiled end writhed, twisted and threw itself toward him. Marin, who had watched the thing with a half-paralyzed blankness, recalled shudderingly his night a week before when a shining rope had extended from the clock in Trask's apartment.

He was tremendously shaken. What the torture had not achieved in affecting him mentally, the luminous rope was accomplishing with every spasmodic leap it made. He watched it with a fascinated horror as it made its peculiar looping, convulsive gesture and then lashed out – three feet nearer.

It had been only twenty-five feet away to begin with. It had covered half that distance in less than two minutes, and after his first shocked reaction, Marin shouted for help. The sound of his voice rose from a call to a yell to the loudest scream he could utter. He had no pride, no impulse to restrain himself. He wanted someone to come and stop what was happening, and he wanted it immediately.

No one came. There was not a sound outside his door. As he realized that no help was coming, Marin had a flash picture of the truth of what was here. The Brain had 'controlled' the Great Judge, evidently in some subtle way, and directed the dictator to put him in a room with a clock. Somehow, then, it had been rationalized that no guard was needed. Or perhaps, even there, it was a case of another slave of the Brain being selected to be a guard.

What was it Slater had said? . . . Control from a distance. That could mean perception of hearing shut off at the key moment, the man simply standing there, unaware of the shouting from inside the room he was guarding.

There was no time for further speculation as to why he was doomed. A shining 'rope' of light reared above his chair, poised uncertainly, and then, as he tried to shrink away, fell across his knees.

From somewhere near by came the sound of ocean surf. There was a pause; and then a solid pack of water tumbled over him. It was so real that he felt himself lifted and buoyantly swept back.

The waters began to recede, and, as the sea washed and trilled and murmured as it flowed back past him, he did something. His mouth closed over a tiny delicacy which the sea had brought to him. And as he swallowed it, he managed to settle down on the sand. Just how he did that was not clear. There was a body action involved, but no thought or awareness – simply doing, being, living.

And then the sea was gone past him, off out of sight. From the near distance came the sound of the surf, bubbling, a faint mumble of many liquid movements, a rolling and hissing and . . .

The sound faded, and was gone.

Marin thought, staggered, I was a sea creature, far back along the evolutionary line. I had a memory from the beginning of life.

An afterthought came, wonderingly: This is what the Pripps do. They can remember such things consciously.

He had an intense feeling of excitement as darkness closed over him. Abruptly, everything grew bright. It was a brightness that irritated. It was from the brightness, he realized, that the excitement derived.

Time passed, and it grew dark. The excitement faded to a vague pulsing. After a while the brightness returned, and with it the feeling of – he knew what it was now – aliveness!

The cycle of light and dark, with its attendant 'emotional' turmoil, repeated many times; and then he had an impression of what it was: life in its most primitive form. Marin felt a private excitement as that awareness touched him. The darkness was night; the brightness, day, sunlight irritating what must in that distant beginning of things have been matter one step removed from inanimateness.

He was still striving to savor it when . . .

He was crouching behind a rocky ridge; and the feeling of excitement was strong, but it was tainted with fear. Something was beyond and below the ridge – something big; and he was afraid, and desperately hoped that it would not become aware of him.

In a spasm of anxiety, his hands closed over the wooden handle of a primitive stone ax. And Marin grew aware that he was no small being as he knelt tensely there on this mountain side. He *felt* rather than saw that his shoulders and chest bulged with huge muscles. He even had the conviction that he could give a good account of himself against the monster beyond the ridge. But it was a senseless creature, massive and stubborn; and it would recoil many times from his blows. Yet in the end it would very likely claw and hug him to death. On his part he could only hope to drive it off; he could not expect to destroy it.

Desperately, he crouched. Anxiously, he hoped to avoid a battle. The change occurred while he was feeling the anxiety.

He was lying in darkness on a carpeted floor. That is, it seemed to be, but it felt slightly different, somehow. He was weaker physically; that was a feeling, visceral, neural, muscular. He thought tensely, Have I been switched to another body?

He attempted to move, and chains rattled, thin, hard rope tightened on his wrists, awareness came of metal bands around his ankles. He relaxed, chilled; and beside him the voice of Riva Allen said, 'Are you awake? How long have we been here?'

Marin tried to think of this now as a dream. For her voice could only be coming out of some converted form of his memory. Riva was dead – disintegrated by the most colossal bomb exploded in a quarter of a century.

Her voice came again, apparently from the night beside him. 'We've been fed eight times. That could be three days. But I feel hungry all the time, so it could be longer.'

Now Marin identified that feeling of physical weakness: hunger. But how could that be? Who was this lying here in a dark room beside a woman who he knew no longer existed?

Shaken, he remembered: I'm here – wherever here is – because of the Brain. Its purposes have nothing to do with my welfare. It wants to know how Wade Trask is dangerous to it and its goals. And so, it is using its knowledge of the function of life to do whatever it's doing.

What has it found out?

A sound interrupted his tense thought. A door opened, admitting a widening shaft of light. Marin turned his head and saw that two Pripp males were entering. They carried steaming dishes on two trays.

Beside Marin, Riva Allen said happily, 'We eat again.' As she spoke, a third individual came through the door. He was masked, and therefore it was not possible to determine by appearance alone if he also was a Pripp. He spoke, and Marin instantly recognized Ralph Scudder's voice.

From behind his mask, the small man said, 'All right, Group Master David Marin, I've decided to release you and your friend.' He turned to the other Pripps. 'Remove their bonds!' he ordered.

Marin was remembering how Scudder had delayed him the night of the explosion with questions. That could explain much. He could guess that Pripp henchmen had been over at Trask's apartment searching. What it didn't explain was: how had they found the secret laboratory?

With an effort, Marin caught himself out of the confusion of speculation. His attention fastened on the one relevant phrase Scudder had used: '*Group Master David Marin.*' That, and only that, mattered.

Marin thought shakily, I'm myself again.

Somehow, the Brain, in doing what it had done, had triggered vital neural mechanisms. In abrupt, intense excitement, he had the thought once more, in all its wonderful meaning: I'm back in my own body!

Scudder was speaking again. 'It was announced a few minutes ago that Wade Trask is in custody. No point in holding you any longer.'

And that explained a lot. The Pripp leader had been loyally waiting for Trask to come. Marin rubbed the circulation back into his arms, ate his share of the food, and gradually came to a decision. It was too soon to draw any conclusions concerning what had happened to him. There were contradictions that could not be resolved by speculation.

The two of them were presently taken to the surface by what was obviously a circuitous route. Marin immediately called the Great Judge's private number from a phone booth. Selis, his excellency's private secretary, came on, went away, and then came back. She seemed shaken.

She said in a low voice, 'David, his excellency refuses to talk to you, but he wants you to be at the council meeting tomorrow morning, at eleven.'

She said in an even lower tone, 'Is there any message you'd like me to give him?'

Marin said uneasily, 'My dear, please ask him not to execute Wade Trask until I have talked to him.'

'Just a moment.' She went away again. When she came back, she was obviously speaking within the dictator's hearing, for she said in a clear but neutral voice, 'He says that Trask has already, by himself, achieved a reprieve until after tomorrow morning's meeting. He says that he cannot understand how a disguised Trask could have won the Jorgian war, and that he will absolutely require a satisfactory explanation. That is all. Good-by.'

There was a click.

CHAPTER THIRTY-FOUR

Outside, walking along in the street, with Riva beside him, Marin shivered a little with the memory of what the dictator's private secretary had said.

He shook his head uneasily. And then he stopped, and, thinking, looked at the girl. She had spent five days with Trask. . . . What had Trask told her?

It seemed to him that he needed more data than he now had if he expected to show up well at the council meeting. He needed every bit of information he could get.

'Want to come with me?' he asked the girl.

She was a thin, haunted-eyed version of slender Riva Allen. But she nodded, and she said, 'You know what that means? You know what I am.'

'Yes, yes,' Marin said, nodding.

He presumed she meant sex. But that was all right. He wanted from her the full story of what had happened — every word, every innuendo. And for that he would pay her the price she required.

He took Riva to his apartment in the great Group Masters' building. He had been aware of a developing irritation in his eyes, but his vision was clear enough. Whatever visual problem Trask had inflicted on the Marin body, it had evidently cleared up easily this time. A tension remained. It was something to take note of.

He was a man who had many things to do. And so he left the woman in his apartment and walked to an elevator that took him down to his office in the Armed Forces section. There he called the chief of Military Intelligence in Jorgia.

The officer said, 'David, I'm awfully glad you called. It's about that private instruction you gave me. We resolved the problem by picking up everybody who tried to cross the border, and have already got some interesting interrogations to report. First, this Wade Trask case, which has been in the news, is not what it seems. They've been holding off because of some secret he had, and they planted one of their top woman agents on him, and—'

Marin was not easily surprised. But now he said involuntarily, 'They *what*!'

'I've been feeling very anxious about this, sir,' said the Intelligence chief. 'I'm very glad you called.'

Marin drew a deep breath. 'Thank you, Colonel. Leave this matter to me.'

'If you hadn't called, I planned to contact his excellency, the Great Judge.'

'Keep me advised of further developments,' Marin said steadily.

As he broke the connection, he realized that he was trembling. Riva Allen! he was thinking. All that time in the apartment — what had she heard? And the days she had spent bound hand and foot on the floor beside a man she believed to be David Marin, a Group Master who was somehow associated with Wade Trask — what had she learned?

Still shaky, he called Communications. He asked the officer

on the swing shift, 'Major, is it possible for anyone to send secret messages out of this building?'

The chunky little man at the other end of the television connection seemed taken aback. 'Sir,' he stuttered, 'that's a big order.' He controlled himself, grew thoughtful. 'A Group Master might do it.'

Marin was astonished, abruptly angry. 'I understood there was an automatic jamming mechanism for all except official communications.' His tone was challenging.

The officer, on the tele-screen, looked shaken. But his voice was steady enough. 'That is correct, sir,' he said, 'unless someone introduces the Trask infinite-series equipment. Most Group Masters have such equipment in their personal apartments – against our advice. We can monitor such messages, but we cannot stop them.'

Marin was nodding, remembering. The Great Judge had wanted a direct line to his councilors. Marin said, 'I want quick action on this. Have the equipment in *my* apartment cut from the power circuits immediately. Don't waste a minute!'

'*Yessir!*'

As Marin broke the connection, his mind had already leaped on to the next possibility. 'Scudder must be in on it – leaving her there beside me for so many days.'

He no sooner had the thought than he was calling the military police. He ordered the arrest of Ralph Scudder, Pripp leader. He instructed: 'Tell Scudder to bring along the map of the Shelters which Wade Trask asked him to prepare. If he co-operates with us, nothing will happen to him. Tell him that.' He finished: 'Hold Scudder for me to question first thing in the morning. Don't let anyone get at him.'

He called Liaison and instructed them to order his son, David Burnley, flown to the capital, to report to his office at 10:40 A.M. the following morning. 'Tell him to wear his lieutenant's uniform.'

He called, next, Major General Eugene Inskip, Retired. Surprisingly, after a brief discussion with a nurse, he was put through to the old man, who said, 'These blasted women get me to bed when the sun goes down. What can I do for you, sir?'

Marin said, 'General, has anyone from my department contacted you in the last day or so?'

The negative answer he received to that was *not* surprising, not really. He had been exposed as an 'impostor' almost immediately after instructing his aide to contact Inskip, and the man had evidently felt himself free to ignore the orders of the false Marin.

Marin drew a deep breath and asked the decisive question: 'Have you completed your book on weapons of the last century?'

There was silence at the other end, then a sigh, and then: 'Young man, I don't know what's on your mind, but I sense an urgent note in your voice. Would you like me to send over a copy of my manuscript?'

Marin said, 'I would not only like to have it, but I'd like to come over for it personally, if you could remain awake and talk to me for a half hour.'

'I'll stay awake the entire blasted night, if it's important – and just let these women try to get me to sleep before you get here.'

Marin laughed softly. 'Good man!' he said. 'Now, listen. What I'm interested in – urgently – are weapons that can affect entire cities, or areas. We're prepared for the big bombs – three quarters of the population are still underground. What else is there?'

'There's a vibration instrument,' said the old man, 'and a gas that has no parallel since and – but I get the idea. I'll look over the material here. There are at least five major weapons in the category you mentioned. I'll be seeing you, sir.'

That took an hour and a half of his vital evening. En route, he ordered the entire technical staff stationed in the Judge's City to report for special duty immediately.

On the way back to his apartment, Marin decided against exposing to Riva his knowledge of her true identity. It wasn't a feeling of mercy. He guessed that the casually murdered body of the true Riva Allen probably lay buried in some concealed grave. No – his lips tightened – it wasn't mercy.

But he knew the possibilities of evasion that were available to the woman. In spite of any attempt to prevent her, she might hastily swallow a drug, and so fatefully delay being questioned.

And so, he'd have to worm it out of her. He had to be adroit. Act as if she were exactly what she pretended to be. It wouldn't matter what *she* learned.

As he entered the apartment, he heard water running in the bathroom. She came out, presently, wearing one of his bathrobes, and she squealed as she saw him and came racing over like a young animal.

Marin returned her kisses cynically, but he recognized that her warmth was not all acting. There was a strong, driving passion in this woman, and he did not doubt but that he would have to satisfy it.

As he undressed, Marin toyed with the idea of using hypnotic gas on her. He rejected that quickly. The gas had a profound effect on other women. It might produce an even longer delay than drugs.

'. . . And then you said . . . And then I said . . .'

The woman had at first resisted giving him a detailed account. She was perceivably puzzled. She kept assuming that he had been there on the floor beside her, and that he must know what their conversations had been about. She would repeat a statement, and then she would look at him there in the dim light of the bedroom and shake her head, as much as to say, 'Surely you don't want to hear *that* again.' So then she would condense and generalize, and, wonderingly, would permit him to wheedle from her the exact words and the precise meaning.

She must be thinking furiously, Marin realized. But she also never forgot her role. Her recall was hindered by a frequent, rising sexual excitement. Or perhaps even that was calculated to discover how urgently he wanted the information, and to what he listened most carefully. She blackmailed him with a candor that would have won his admiration under other circumstances.

But he kept reiterating the rationalization which he had offered as explanation for his detailed questioning: he had been in a partially drugged state – that was his story – and he wanted to know what their captor might have learned from him. Because of the drug, his recollections were vague.

So he maintained, and so he kept repeating. And, gradually, he realized that, although Trask had uttered the kind of indiscretions that came under the heading of 'loose talk' and had talked about his social ideas, and made veiled references to his invention, the invention itself was too radical. People just couldn't of themselves make the mind-leap necessary to grasping the concepts of mechanical interchange of personality that were involved. He guessed, with relief, that in these many days this spy had learned nothing.

At about 4:00 A.M. the woman fell into what seemed to be an exhausted sleep. Marin waited until her breathing was even and slow. Then he slipped out of the bed and went to the outer corridor to check if guards were stationed at his door, as he had ordered. They were, two of them, both women – physically powerful, trained agents of Military Intelligence.

'Wake her at eight-thirty,' he instructed, 'take her to your department, and have her questioned.'

With that, he took his clothes and headed for his office. He lay down on a cot in a little room that adjoined. And there, for a while, he lay awake, restless and disturbed.

The night had not been wasted. What had seemed to be wholly disconnected events fitted together. And Marin quailed before their tremendous meaning. If this is true, he thought shakily, if this is true . . .

Then he thought, Trask and I have been like two lambs wandering through a slaughterhouse.

As his tired eyes finally flickered shut, he was thinking wearily, Now, I've *got* to decide!

CHAPTER THIRTY-FIVE

Shortly after 6:00 A.M. Marin got up, slipped into his dressing gown, and phoned Colonel Gregson, the Deputy Master on duty. A sleepy voice came on the line. 'Gregson speaking.'

Marin identified himself, and said, 'Is Scudder in custody?'

'Yes. We've got him.' The colonel was alert now. 'He was really surprised.'

Marin could imagine. So much secretiveness so abruptly exposed. But all he said was, 'Bring him to my office right away.'

'With the map?'

'With the map. And, Greg!'

'Yes?'

'I want attack squads available, with heavy-duty equipment to break through barriers. It'll be in the Shelters, so use explosive demolition sparingly.'

'We'll take gas, and some radiation stuff.'

'Fine.'

'Have it all ready by nine?'

'Yes.'

'It shall be done!' said Gregson.

Marin broke the connection and called Air Defense. 'Issue instructions to the Air Control forces to permit no flying machines to enter the city until further notice. Maintain a watch to the upper limits of altitude. Shoot on sight on the upper limits of altitude. Shoot on sight on the upper levels, and after brief warning at various lower levels. And, Mayer!'

'Yes, sir?'

'Call no one on this. Advise the day personnel as they arrive on the job.'

'Very well, sir.'

Marin broke the connection and stood up. And then, for the first time, he realized how great a change there was in him. Sometime during the brief sleep he had had, there in the night, he had made up his mind. He knew what he must do. Knew it with a profound purposefulness, and on a level of certainty that far transcended anything he had ever known.

He was prepared to act – without *boundaries*.

Out of the events and the turmoil, a man had been born. He looked back at a career that was half violence, half ideals, and all conformance. He had lived his life in a framework whereby he had agreed to accept the world of the Great Judge.

All that was over. Doubt was ended, fear gone. As Marin dressed, he considered what he must do on this day of decision. And there was no doubt. Everything was sharp and clear in his mind. And obvious.

It would be a battle of a peculiar kind. Since he had, for the moment, anyway, enormous military power under his control, he could make moves against the hidden adversary. Somewhere along the line, the adversary – in this case, the Brain – would have to start fighting back.

The circumstances of the struggle were fantastic. At any moment the Brain might seize mental control of all its principal antagonists. Under such circumstances, he needed only one thing: the determination to act, to set forces in motion, and so compel a reaction.

Act – regardless of consequences.

Marin walked to his office along corridors that were almost deserted at this hour of the morning. He had breakfast sent from the officer's commissary, and he was eating it when Scudder was brought in, a snarling, anxious little man. 'So Trask talked,' he said grimly. 'Well, I did nothing but agree to provide him with a map. What's illegal about that?'

Marin said curtly, 'Where's the map?'

Colonel Gregson had it. He was a modest, sturdy man in his early forties. He spread the map out on a stand, so that lights could be focused on it. Marin motioned to the Pripp.

'Explain it,' he said.

Scudder did so, sullenly. It turned out that the significant levels of the Shelters were the forty-eighth, forty-ninth, fiftieth and fifty-first. Military maps of the area indicated that these areas had been sealed off for a quarter of a century by order of the Great Judge.

And still the Brain seemed unaware that David Marin was planning against it. Marin had another moment of tension. But his voice was steady as he gave the order that sent the attack squads to seize the areas outlined by the maps and destroy any machinery or instrument they found. Destroy it, smash it, burn it, leave no working part in commission. It disturbed him to give so destructive an order. But he saw no alternative.

He had the feeling that no one now alive – except possibly Wade Trask – knew enough. And Trask was not available.

When the orders were given, and the men were on their way, he sent a Signal regiment on hopjets – on the double – to all telephone sub-stations, with orders to cut off the phone service from the entire area of Pripp City, and of all lines leading into the Shelters.

Stop all long-distance calls. . . .

CHAPTER THIRTY-SIX

And that's it! Marin thought.

He felt ever so slightly let down. But he had started the main forces in motion. There was nothing to do but wait.

While he waited, he sat in his office and exercised his great power as a member of the inner council and as a government leader. He sent out to key television and radio stations an announcement to be broadcast at 11:00 A.M. that he was resigning as a Group Master.

He had his official ring packaged, and he personally addressed it to 'My beloved Delindy' at her midwest retreat. His seal of office, he wrapped up himself and sent to the messenger department with instructions to deliver it to Selis at the Judge's Court at eleven-fifteen. He prepared letters to be sent to the office of each Group Master announcing his relinquishment of all of his official positions.

He placed his military decorations in their jeweled case and sent them by messenger to the keeper of honors at the military cemetery. He could not resign from his group, so he made no contact with them.

At twenty to ten, his private speaker roared with the voices of squad leaders communicating with each other.

There was a pregnant pause. Then the hissing sound of a mobile gas fire unit reverberated from the speaker.

Marin turned down the volume. And then, as the sounds continued, he shut off the instrument.

His phone rang.

His secretary called from the outer office, 'Colonel Gregson calling from a field telephone, sir.'

Gregson said, 'David, we seem to be fighting two forces. When we approach from one direction, we run into Pripps. From all other directions, it's a mechanical monster with massive metal walls: our instruments measure eight feet of thickness. Both the Pripps and the machine are fighting us with gas units, and it's tough going.'

Marin said, with satisfaction, 'You've stirred up the hornet's nest. Keep firing.'

He broke the connection and had Scudder brought in again. The Pripp was defiant.

'I'm innocent,' Scudder protested, 'but I know what's going on. We – that is, us – those of us down there in the Shelters can hold you off for a week. We're bargaining.'

Unexpected statement! 'Bargaining!' said Marin blankly. Then: 'For heaven's sake – with whom?'

'With the real rulers of the world!' said Scudder defiantly. He added, with a sneer, 'And you'd better not pass that information around without asking permission from your lord and master, the Great Judge.'

For Marin, who had already burned his bridges, what was interesting was that the secret was being brought into the open from still another quarter. Inwardly bracing himself, he said now, mildly, 'Are you going to tell me the details?'

'It's real simple,' said Scudder. 'My suspicion began when I was approached and told that I would shortly be asked to supply Pripps for the Great Judge's bodyguard. A while back, that was. We Pripps had two bosses then – the Great Judge, and the agents of this secret group. Know who paid me most? The group did. And so we had our first big "in". About there, Trask began to come around. He had a theory that Pripps were not an accident, not a product of war. I saw right away that, if we could prove that, we might get the limitations of our movements removed. So I played along with him, and I began to check back in the old records. I learned enough to convince me that it was an experiment in its early stages, and that it was this secret group that did it.'

He went on, grimly: 'So that's what we're bargaining for. We want data on those experiments.'

He was a small caricature of a man. But Marin saw in him all the determination of a human being fighting for his life. He visualized a week's delay in the destruction of the Brain. And shuddered. And knew that he also must bargain with everything he had.

On that level, he felt no mercy. For shortly after eleven o'clock, he would cease to have the power to do anything on a government level.

He began: 'You're bargaining with the wrong people. I'm the person you should be dealing with, because – listen!' In an even voice, he described the arrests that were being made in Jorgia, and the interrogations that were taking place. He finished: 'Briefly, bluntly, if you do not contact your associates in command down in the Shelters, I shall order your execution within the hour. If they do not surrender by ten-thirty, every Pripp eventually captured will be executed. Now, don't argue with me. Just say yes or no.'

The small rat face was livid, but there was still courage there. He said, 'What about the data on the Pripp experiments?'

'All information which results from the interrogations on that subject,' Marin promised, 'will be turned over to the Pripps.'

Scudder was silent. He sat, staring at the floor, his small body hunched up. He straightened with a faint sound, like a suppressed snarl. 'All right,' he said sullenly. 'We'll surrender.'

The victory had overtones of tragedy in it, and Marin resolved inwardly that he would in the future take an interest in these shattered people. If anything could be done, it should be.

But there was another question in his mind. How had his body been taken out of Trask's secret laboratory over to Scudder's hide-out? He asked the question.

Scudder said, 'Yes, my men took your body from the laboratory. About an hour before the bomb, that was.' He laughed grimly. 'Funny thing, I had Trask in my office, and I was holding him there to give the men a better chance to search Trask's apartment.'

'But why search his place?' asked Marin. 'You didn't expect to find me, did you?'

Scudder shook his head. 'No, you don't owe us any gratitude. You were just lucky. The woman – what's her name, Riva Allen – called me through the secret channels of the people who are behind her. She'd been watching Trask for days, and he kept disappearing into his den. She was baffled.'

'Thank you,' said Marin.

He was enormously relieved to hear the facts at last. Riva Allen was brought in. She entered the room with an air. She seemed intelligent, assured and quite gay. She had obviously abandoned her act of being an unregistered courtesan. She looked at Marin with a bright smile and said cheerfully, 'Well – *lover*!' And she laughed, an easy, tinkling, relaxed laughter.

Marin glanced questioningly at the women who had escorted his captive. He recognized them as skillful interrogators. He asked, 'Get anything?'

The older woman answered, 'We've been with her ever since she was turned over to us at a quarter to nine. Everything we ask her, every persuasive method we use, just makes her laugh.'

Marin nodded calmly. But there was no doubt of the defeat that was here. His guess the night before had been correct. Chemicals. Most likely she had had the stuff concealed in a false tooth, which simply required her to bite down once, hard. He knew this 'laughing' drug. It ended all fear. Threat of death, use of torture were equally funny to the individual under its influence. The effect would last about twenty-four hours. By taking such a drug, this woman spy had removed herself as a participant during the decisive hours ahead.

Marin said, reluctantly but with finality, 'Take her away! Keep her under arrest!'

His secretary came in. 'Lieutenant David Burnley to see you, sir, by your instructions.'

Marin said, 'Send him in.'

CHAPTER THIRTY-SEVEN

The boy came through the door; he was a towering figure, massively filling his blue and yellow uniform. He came to a halt, brought himself to attention, and saluted.

Marin said, deliberately, 'Hello, Son.'

He felt slightly ashamed at the effect the words had on the other. Ashamed because of his own purpose. He needed the kind of loyalty in the next hour that was not available from just anyone. It was the kind of loyalty that a father might expect from his son. He saw that the boy's face reflected strong emotions and that his greeting had had the desired reaction.

'Hello . . . Dad,' said David Burnley. 'You sent for me?'

'I'm very happy to see you,' said Marin. The feeling of shame and guilt was gone. What he was about to do was so necessary that any compunction at this late hour was ridiculous. He went on: 'I have a very important mission for you.'

'It will be an honour.'

Marin had previously decided to make no explanation. He said now, 'Come with me, David!' and started for the door. Then he paused, and turned. 'You're going to be in charge of a detail of soldiers. Don't let on to them that you're my son.'

'Very good, sir.' The big youth's face was firm. He saluted.

Marin said quietly, 'I'm placing great trust in you on a very important matter.'

David Burnley swallowed. But when he spoke, his voice was under control. 'You can count on me, sir.'

'I do, Lieutenant,' said Marin.

They spoke no more. He turned again, and this time he led the way through the outer office to the corridor outside. He had earlier directed that a dozen first-class privates and a corporal be sent from local command. As he had every right to expect, they were waiting at ease. Marin introduced 'Lieutenant David Burnley, the officer who will be your commander until further notice.'

He then gave precise instructions as to what he wanted them to do. Here, again, he made no explanations. They were trained soldiers. He was their commander-in-chief. He had not looked directly at his son while he addressed the men. But from the corner of one eye he had observed the color drain from his cheeks. Now he faced the boy. 'Lieutenant!'

'Yes, sir!'

'Take charge of your men and follow me!'

'Yes, sir!'

They took an elevator to the floor where the council meeting would begin at eleven sharp. Marin glanced at his watch. Four and a half minutes to the hour. This was timing with a vengeance.

There were five Pripp guards and a Pripp officer at the council room door as Marin came up. Their presence indicated that the Great Judge had already arrived. The officer nodded his recognition of Marin and said, 'We'll have to search you as usual, sir!'

'Naturally,' said Marin. And he pressed the trigger of the gas gun in his pocket.

He caught the officer with one hand and fired past him at one of the guards. From behind him, the men were already discharging their weapons. There was no real fight. The surprise was too complete. The six Pripps went down before the unexpected attack.

Marin did not wait to see what transpired. He entered the conference room without a single glance behind him. As the door closed, he noticed by the clock on the wall that faced the door that it was one minute after eleven. And that his timing was still perfect.

CHAPTER THIRTY-EIGHT

Standing just inside the door of the brilliantly lighted conference room, Marin permitted the dictator's bodyguard hidden behind peepholes in the walls to look him over, to recognize him, mentally to lower their 'guard.' Waited while the soldiers whom he had given their commands stole up the staircase that led to the peephole area and worked their second surprise attack.

As he waited, he walked slowly toward where the Great Judge stood beside Podrage. And now he was beginning to feel the strain. For there was a critical moment coming, again a matter of timing. The soldiers were supposed to render the peephole guards unconscious with gas weapons and then take over the peephole weapons – and protect him. The critical point was that he didn't want them to recognize the dictator before the decisive moment.

'. . . thirteen, fourteen, fifteen!' he counted.

In that instant before he acted, the entire scene was vividly etched in Marin's brain: the assembled Group Masters, with only Medellin and the redoubtable Edmund Slater missing; Wade Trask manacled to a chair at one end of the table; and the Great Judge immaculate in white suit and blouse, in the process of turning to glance at Marin.

Now! thought Marin. He fired his special hypnotic gas gun,

again through his pocket, aiming for the dictator's head. The beam, though it was only a few molecules thick, caused the other's head to jerk slightly back. It must have seemed like a muscular twitch, for the Great Judge showed no sign of having felt it.

Marin waited. The gas was viruslike, but faster than any virus. Within instants it permeated the rivers of blood flowing through the brain. The sensitive neuron cells began to respond to its presence, giving up the potassium held in suspension on the electrified surface of each cell – or, rather, suspended in the energy field which *was* the surface of each cell. Instant change – thoughts, emotions, the bonds that held the personality, the ego, integrated into a unified whole lost their immense cohesive strength.

The dictator staggered and started to sink down. Podrage and Marin together caught the limp body and prevented a fall.

'Over here!' said Marin.

They placed the Great Judge in the armchair at the head of the table. Although his head drooped to one side, he looked relaxed rather than unconscious, and so the soldiers, who must just now be taking their places at the peepholes, might wonder, but they couldn't know.

Marin gave that aspect only the most fleeting thought. The moment the dictator was safely in the chair, he let go, and turned – just as men began to recover from the first surprise.

Somebody said hoarsely, 'Get a doctor! He's fainted.'

Momentarily, that startled Marin. It hadn't occurred to him that the confusion would be so complete.

He saw that Group Master John Peeler was in the act of opening the outer door. And guessed grimly that the secret would be out in a moment.

A gas gun poked almost into Peeler's face. He reeled back in surprise, as a soldier's voice simultaneously announced, and every word was clearly audible, 'We have orders from General Marin to permit no one out of this room.'

From where he stood, Marin said, 'Soldier, shut the door.'

'*Yes, sir!*'

The door closed.

CHAPTER THIRTY-NINE

Men were turning and staring at Marin. Most of the faces Marin glanced at were stunned with a hint of fear. Overlying the fear was anger.

Group Master Yarini said savagely, 'For that action alone' – he pointed at the Great Judge's limp body – 'you will go to the Converter.'

Marin grew aware that the formidable Podrage was studying him. The man said, finally, oddly, 'What are you up to, David?'

The verbal reactions indicated that the first shock was over. So Marin said, 'Calm your fears, gentlemen. This is not a *coup d'état*. But I require your full attention while I explain what it is.'

They started silently to walk toward their seats at the conference table. Abruptly, there was sound. Group Master Yarini, instead of sitting, grasped at his chair, lifted it and, with a yell, bore down at Marin.

He took two steps, then he began to stumble. Then he fell in a heap. The faint odor of a gas rifle discharge permeated the air and was gone.

If he had not already guessed that his men were in control of the peepholes, Marin knew it now. He said quietly, 'Gentlemen, do not deny yourself the privilege of hearing my story. The Great Judge will awaken presently, so there is no need to worry about him.'

For a time, then, they listened, silently, uneasily. Marin guessed some of them were wondering if their willingness to be an audience was not somehow compromising. But he was prepared to force them to listen; so let them have their doubts and their fears.

He began his account with a description of his first visit to Trask, when he had been forced into a switch of identity. He gave the entire story of his association with Trask, and then – and not until then – named the Great Judge as the unsuspected protector and agent of the Brain.

At that point, John Peeler jerked his hands up and placed

them over his ears. He was pale. He shouted, 'I refuse to listen to another word of this fantastic treason.'

Marin snatched his gas gun, shot him, watched him slump, and then said coldly to the others, 'In my opinion, Peeler and Yarini are making a play for the Great Judge. If you can tolerate such cowards at future sessions of the Group Masters Council, you will merit contempt.'

Group Master Elstan said grimly, 'You won't be around, David, to see who's at the council meetings.'

Marin said, 'You are quite right.' He described in an even tone how he had resigned publicly from the council before coming to the meeting.

Podrage looked at him, shook his head wonderingly and said, 'May I call my office and check on that?'

Marin nodded, and waited while Podrage picked up his personal phone, and waited while he asked the question. The group master hung up finally and glanced around the room. He was visibly nonplussed. He said finally, slowly, 'The total news announcement by David has caused a sensation. The stock market has already declined several points.'

Group Master Elstan jumped to his feet. All thought of treason and sedition seemed gone from his mind. 'I must call my broker!' he muttered.

He fumbled for the phone on the outjut of the desk beside him. Marin said, in abrupt fury, 'Sit down! Stop disgracing yourself!'

The older man hesitated, flushed, and then sat without another word.

Podrage climbed to his feet. 'David,' he said, 'may I ask how you account for the fact that the Brain did not do any body switching, after learning how?'

Marin was momentarily silent – but there was no escape from the theory by which he was operating. He started to speak, hesitated, and then said, 'In my opinion – and I should point out that this opinion is based on the Brain's failure to take action against me – it knows nothing about that. I believe that when it . . . contacted . . . the imprisoned Wade Trask – meaning myself – it accidentally stimulated a neural mechanism which automatically caused a readjustment of identity. And I further believe that it was baffled by the phenomenon.'

He added thoughtfully, 'That was not my first feeling.'

Podrage said, 'This is conjecture only.'

Marin inclined his head yes. But he was irritated by what seemed to him the inability of everyone present to see how he was forcing the facts out into the open.

When he spoke, his voice was steady. 'It is only conjecture, but the logic of it is being proved by the Brain's failure to take preventive action against me. The truth – whatever it is – will be proved completely before the end of the day.'

Podrage persisted: 'You mean, now that you've put it under pressure, it will have to prove what it can do?'

Marin started to answer with an impatient comment on the obviousness of that. He stopped himself. It struck him that Podrage, in thus having him give his account in its most elementary terms, was trying to help him.

He had a sudden realization of this situation. These men were actually still in a state of shock. They needed a simple story simply told.

'Yes,' he said resonantly. 'Yes, Mr. Podrage. Is there any other point you would like clarified?'

Podrage looked at him steadily for a moment, and there was a faint smile on his strong face. He parted his lips, but before he could speak, he was interrupted by many voices. For a moment it seemed as if everyone present was speaking at the same time.

'The Brain was clever once. How do we know it won't outsmart us again? . . . What will happen when his excellency awakens? . . . What do *you* plan to do? . . . How will we know when the Brain is really defeated? . . . What? . . .'

Marin held up his hand. When the clamor did not subside, he raised his voice, admonishing, 'Genlemen, *please*!'

That stopped them. Podrage gravely broke the silence: 'I think, David, what that medley of questions indicates more than anything else is: what will happen when' – he nodded at the unconscious Great Judge – 'comes to? I believe sincerely that part of the anger you have seen is rooted in anxiety over your fate. That may surprise you.'

Marin allowed his glance to turn in the direction of the dictator. He was thinking, What a remarkable man was here. Beyond all doubt the Great Judge retained the loyalty of his ministers. His personality transcended any revelation of weakness that might be made about him.

His second thought took a different turn. It was more personal. For the first time since early that morning, he thought, What *will* become of me? He had burned all his bridges. Standing here, he was an ordinary citizen, without legal powers, and subject to any and all penalties that might result from what he was now doing.

The uneasy feeling passed as swiftly as it had come. He said steadily, 'We have a strange story to hear before we come to my fate. When I began to suspect the real truth last night, I realized that I was sitting in the wings watching a drama the existence of which I had not even suspected. I realized, too, that in a way I knew this all before. You see, gentlemen, all the apparently unrelated data fit: the Brain, the setting up of many states after the war, the quick surrender of most of them when we challenged their right to exist, the innumerable executions, and we mustn't forget the continued physical well-being of his excellency ... And now I'd like to give you a glimpse of this astonishing scene.'

He walked over to the Great Judge's chair, pulled up one of the near-by chairs for himself, sat down, and said, 'Your excellency, you are now free to speak to me. You *want* to speak to me. Do you understand?'

The dictator seemed to straighten. 'I understand,' he said.

There was a fluttering sound of movement among the listeners. Marin heard, but did not look around.

CHAPTER FORTY

Marin said, 'How old are you?'

Somebody said, *sotto voce,* 'My God!'

The Great Judge answered, 'Seventy-nine.'

Marin glanced quickly around the long table. The faces he saw were a study in fascinated attention. There was no question but that the first fact he had adduced was a sensation.

He turned back to the Great Judge, and question by question drew out the rest of the strange and powerful tale.

The story was:

During the third atomic war, he was a liaison officer attached to the general staff of the Combined Eastern Powers. He knew most of the secrets and most of the capable men in every sector: scientists, field men, research workers and a host of technically skilled individuals. Toward the end of the cataclysmic war, he became aware that there was a plot among the scientists and that research men everywhere were in a state of intellectual ferment. Some great ideas were in motion. Wartime research had brought forth new inventions and new discoveries, in all fields. There was, particularly, a discovery that had to do with slowing the processes of aging, and even to some extent rejuvenation of already aged tissues.

Many other little-known discoveries offered the greatest possibility of exploitation by a determined group.

Colonel Ivan Prokov saw his unique situation. As the only general staff officer in on the plot, he could virtually name his own terms to the other conspirators.

Marin at that point turned to the assembled Group Masters and said, 'At the proper moment, only a man in Colonel Prokov's liaison position could ensure the capture or execution of the upper-level staff officers.'

No one said anything. He turned back to his hypnotic interrogation. The recount continued.

Liaison had long been established with similar groups among the Allied Western Nations. And so the plot to end the war and take over the world was conceived and carried out with unmatched brilliance.

A tendency to a sort of intense nationalistic schizophrenia had been anticipated, particularly in the east and in the middle east. And so, of the thousand separate states that sprang into being, the majority were taken over by special secret agents of the group. The internal and external pressures in each state were terrific. In some cases, the secret agent, even though he was head of government, had to use every device of treason and trickery to hand his area over to the Union of the Great Judge – to the World State. In most cases, union could only be achieved by a combination of betrayal and war.

Again, Marin paused to comment. 'As you all know, I have for more than a decade conducted these wars. I presume that wherever we executed government leaders, they were *not* members of the conspiratorial group, and where we left them in power – for whatever reason – they were.'

He added, 'with the exception of Jorgia – but we'll come to that.'

The very first echelon of the original plotters had been imbued with the eastern group idea. They were aware of the necessity of making a compromise with the free-enterprise forces, to end the war. But to them it *was* a compromise, and the secret agreement among them was that the Great Judge would presently sabotage the capitalistic economic idea and substitute Socialism based on the groups.

The first step toward liquidation of the compromise was carried out remorselessly, and on schedule. Eighty thousand of the western co-conspirators were executed – with only one setback. The 'Westerners' had, during the war, hidden the 'Brain'.

Ten years later, the Great Judge used the failure to find that mechanical being as a reason for his delay in eliminating free enterprise. And so, the secret group of conspirators, operating out of a series of sham organizations with headquarters in Jorgia, became suspicious of him.

Despite their individual longevity, the conspirators had for years cultivated promising young people. Some of these were admitted into the organization. Others, like Wade Trask, were not trusted in the inner organization, but they proved useful. Trask – who had his own ideas about social changes – was used to discover finally if the Great Judge would or would not co-operate. The dictator was informed through channels that Trask would make seditious utterances about the groups.

Trask was arrested and sentenced to death. . . .

Instantly, the battle was on. The conspirators knew that their worst fears were true. And that the Great Judge was not going to alter the group-free-enterprise compromise.

They had flung down the gauntlet – Trask's sedition. In sentencing Trask to the Converter, the dictator made clear that he was now in total opposition to his former colleagues.

Marin paused to glance at Trask. 'What do you think of all this, Wade?'

The scientist had been staring into space. Now he stirred,

and he said wearily, 'Who would have suspected that the third atomic war is not yet over?'

Marin turned back to the dictator. 'Your excellency, you *want* to tell us, is any one of the conspirators a Group Master?'

'Yes. Yarini and John Peeler.'

'Well!' said Marin, and he glanced around with genuine satisfaction. 'These men were singularly lacking in resourcefulness in their attempts to stop what I'm doing.'

Group Master Elstan said mildly, 'You've got to admit, David, that your surprise was complete.'

Marin scarcely heard. He was asking his next question: 'You want to tell us. . . . How can we capture these . . . Communists, your excellency?'

The answer was drab. 'There's no sure way. All members are usually disguised. They seek out unsuspected persons and study their habits. Then they either kill or shanghai them and take their places.'

'About how many top leaders are there?' Marin asked. 'You want to tell us, sir! I mean, *top* leaders. Inner circle.'

'About three thousand,' said the Great Judge.

'They must have a headquarters,' said Marin, in that urging tone. 'A center through which communication is carried on. You want to tell us.'

'I don't know where it is.'

Marin drew back. He was disappointed. But after a moment, he thought, Only three thousand. That's not so many. Such a small group would, under some circumstances, concentrate in a relatively small area. Like Jorgia. And if they learned too late that an attack was actually to take place, then they would destroy equipment instead of moving it. As they had done and were still doing.

Tensely, Marin asked the question: 'Did you advise the group of the attack on Jorgia, and, if so, when?'

'On the day that Trask was sentenced.'

'That was less advance notice than in the past?'

'Yes. Much less.'

There was an interruption. Group Master Gaines, who had been watching silently with his large, sad eyes, said, 'What I don't understand is why did you feel it necessary to put his excellency into an hypnotic condition? It seems to me he would have told us all this the moment he was confronted with the truth.'

Marin said, 'I'm coming to that.' He turned to the dictator. 'Why did you advise these people?'

'I hoped they would continue to play along with me until we were ready to take over the rest of the world. I wanted them to think the differences between us were not fundamental but a matter of disagreement as to the right time for the change-over.'

'But why play along with them at all?'

'They were threatening to cut me off from the longevity drugs.'

Marin said, 'Oh!' And then he was silent. And then he said, 'Have they?'

'Yes. My usual supply failed to arrive this week.'

Marin glanced at Gaines. 'Does that answer your question, sir?'

'My God . . . yes!'

To the Great Judge, Marin said, 'You want to tell me. Do you know where the Brain is?'

'No.'

And that, it seemed to Marin, made the story complete. And yet, Marin was conscious that his tension was mounting, not lessening. It seemed as if every fact was in, and all necessary action taken. And yet . . .

He saw that Podrage was shaking his head. Podrage said, 'How does the Royal Jorgian government fit into all this? They seem to have been totally innocent.'

Marin nodded. 'They are. The conspirators had forced a western-style government, complete with monarchy, on a people long accustomed to the group idea. The idea, of course, was that such a government would be easy to overthrow. The original "king" had been one of the conspirators before his assassination. His daughters were kept ignorant of this, but their lives were to be spared.'

One of the Group Masters murmured, 'Wheels within wheels within wheels . . .'

Marin said earnestly, 'Any world-wide conspiracy would include an immense number of special situations. There would be experts, and departments, and skilled interpreters. No one person could ever give more than a broad outline, such as we are obtaining now.'

'But the Brain,' said Podrage urgently. 'How does *it* fit into all this?'

Marin had two reactions to the question. First, a return of irritation. Then he recognized the irritation as an expression of his developing anxiety. He said uneasily, 'Something is missing. I feel that we are in profound danger. My impulse is to evacuate the entire city.'

A dead silence fell on the group.

CHAPTER FORTY-ONE

It was Podrage who broke the silence, and for the first time in that prolonged crisis *he* sounded peevish. 'David, is this just a feeling?'

Marin hesitated. He felt mentally gummy and vague. And it was hard even to think about the other man's question. He looked around the room, amazed at how foggy everything was, how far away. The men seemed unreal, the room dim.

Podrage bent over Marin. 'I can't imagine what can go wrong at this stage. Most of the conspirators have been captured. The Brain's hiding place has been found, and it is under direct attack. The city is guarded as never before in history. The only person who might be dangerous if he were under the Brain's control is the Great Judge, and he is protected from any damage that might result from such control. We—' He stopped. His eyes narrowed. 'What's the matter, man?' he asked sharply. 'You look sick.'

That something was wrong was already apparent to Marin. He felt a panic as strong as that he had experienced when, bound hand and foot, he had watched the whiplash luminous rope come toward him from the clock. With a tremendous effort, trembling in every part of his body, he stood up. 'Get me walking!' he said thickly.

Strong hands grabbed him and propelled him. He began to be aware again. Some of the shakiness went out of his legs. He freed himself and stood in the center of the room, swaying a little but fighting that inner sense of farawayness. His feverish gaze fell on Trask.

The scientist was straining against his manacles. The muscles of his neck and lower jaw were taut. His whole body seemed to be tense, and his face was wet with perspiration. His eyes, glazed, apparently unseeing, rolled loosely toward Marin. He stiffened. He said hoarsely, 'David, something has been trying to take control of my mind the last few minutes.'

Around Marin, the shadows deepened again. The room appeared almost dark, and the men in it figures silhouetted as in a dense gloom. His thought went back to his son, David Burnley, who had a 'thing' in his mind. Now he wondered, Is what I'm feeling the same? Is this what it means to have a *thing* in your mind?

It was hard to believe. There was no clear-cut feeling, no thoughts, no sense of another entity taking over. He was more like a man standing in shallow water; he had yet to feel the deep water closing over his head.

That stirred him a second time. He said, fumbling for each word, 'Is there any command?'

'Yes. Something about stopping the attack! I have the feeling that it thinks I'm you.'

And that was such a big idea that it was difficult to grasp all of the potentialities. It meant that the Brain *was* under pressure. And it meant that now, this instant, the Brain was revealing what it knew and what it didn't know.

It didn't know that there had been an identity shift between Trask and himself. What was disturbing was that there must still be *rapport* between Trask and himself. Nothing else could explain the strong feelings he had had and was still having – the dullness, the sense of darkness, the unreality.

He must be catching the overtones of the Brain's energy projection at Trask. Something of Trask remained in him, and something of him in Trask. And yet, if the Brain believed it was dealing with David Marin, it must have taken control of him when he was Trask. But when?

Marin glanced from face to grim face. Then deliberately he took his gas gun from his pocket and set it for a minimum discharge, which was about thirty minutes for an average human being. He said tensely, 'Gentlemen, I had better be questioned. Find out while I'm under if the Brain at any time ever took control of me.'

He seated himself in a chair, raised his weapon, and pressed the trigger.

From his left, Elstan said, 'I don't care for this. You're doing this too fast.'

Marin thought vaguely, Could he be right?

That was all he had time for. His own thought ceased. He seemed to be out in space, drifting through starlit darkness. A voice said, almost directly into his ear – or was it, he wondered, a thought projected into Trask's mind, which he was somehow tuned in upon? – 'You be welcome to this in-full communication. I have kept my own counsel for many years. But now I have communication most important for human species. Humans be not very good thinking people. All human thinking be made illogical by in-a-frame associations. A human have hate for something, he thinking in-a-frame with hate. A human belong to a grouping of other humans, he thinking only in-a-frame with the grouping. All humans have not never understanding of how their thinking did be have its roots. Accordingly, there be no hope for they. They have future only if I helping. Without I, the species be die for sure. I very much now be needing your assist. For your assist, I herewith be offer you my in-full co-operation. My co-operation will make strength for you real powerful. You thinking, I acting. You directing, I doing. You be my master from this time to all your future. Good enough?'

It was a question. But he seemed to be floating, still. The stars were bright. Space was black. His thought drifted to the 'thing' in David Burnley's mind. Was that the Brain? And if so did it at that time co-operate with the conspirators?

'No!' The answer came into his mind. 'I kept my exteroceptors on David Burnley like on all my agents. I see him in danger and give him my protection. Very good I be in control. Two men who find your son in library at military camp hope he will be co-operate. But if he not co-operate they plan to be kill him, and they have someone made up to look like him for substitution. I be take over your son, and make him say, "Okay, fine, I will do what do you wish" – right questions, right answers, no hesitation, no fooling. Good enough, eh?'

The realization that a conversation was possible struck Marin sharply. The reference to 'agents' chilled him. He remembered the atomic bomb that had destroyed the area of Group 814. 'Did you do that?' he asked mentally.

'Yes.'

There was more on that. It had not understood what was happening in Trask's apartment, and since what was occurring there had the 'appear' of danger, 'I destruction.' Human beings, the Brain went on, had many 'offspring,' and these quickly filled up 'the empty spaces killed.' So it didn't really matter how many were exterminated, if a solid core of humanity remained to carry on the race.

The philosophy behind that was too cruel for Marin. 'That's why we're going to destroy you,' he said. 'We don't care for that kind of logic.'

'You talking real foolish' was the answer. 'Typical human emotion thinking. In moments of good feeling, humans talk compassion, and be have apparent logic. Not so. Have hate, logic be twisted. Destruction become senseless, far more cruel than I. I be do what be logical – no more, no less.'

Marin agreed within himself that there was some truth in the Brain's analysis. But the argument did not influence him. He said, 'We're not interested in having a mechanical brain control human beings. You were given the wrong instructions. Clear the problem from your works and await further instructions. That's all I'll say to you.'

The reply was matter-of-fact and grim. 'You be have do what I say. You be under my in-full control. Something not quite clear about why control not work good, but good enough, I think.'

It was either true or it wasn't true. 'I don't think I am under your control, but I'd like to know when you believe you took control of me.'

'In the Shelters.'

The sense of relief that came to Marin had in it a great tiredness. He felt as if he had been under a sustained strain, and now he knew. As Trask, he had been taken over by the Brain during that unwise venture into the Shelters from the Judge's Court. As Marin, he was subject only to whatever extrasensory connection remained between him and the scientist.

Since he had no intention of explaining to the Brain in detail what had happened between himself and Trask, he said, 'I have an idea your control of me is not as good as you believe.'

The Brain said, 'I have to say there be something here which puzzle me. But I give you one more chance. I be instrument of great value. I be have accumulation of one hundred and twenty-five years of data, and value of over one trillion dollars. That's one reason. Another: When I long ago make you my choose for master, I find all your offspring and have they on my control lines. It be bad if I be have kill they all.'

'If you kill any one of them,' Marin retorted, 'then I won't even let you surrender. And besides, what's all this about controlling me through my family. I thought the whole theory behind the mating games was that the family unit was not important.'

'Family always important. But first break old patterns, then establish new ones. Then family again – new way. Hear me, friend. You ending attack, and ending it now – or I be have no choice but destruction entire city. My rules leave me no choice. Think quick!'

There was a pause, a silence, an end of contact. Marin opened his eyes and looked up at the men who were gathered around him. He realized he was smiling but extremely tense. He said, 'Sound the Shelter alarm. I don't know how long we have, but it may only be minutes.'

CHAPTER FORTY-TWO

As Marin climbed to his feet, he saw that it was ten minutes after two.

He stared at the wall clock almost unbelievingly. He had had the feeling that many, many hours had gone by. Telling his story, persuading incredulous men, interrogating the unconscious Great Judge – none of it had been easy. Some of it had seemed interminable. What shocked him was that the attack force under Gregson had had so little time as yet to break through the defenses of the Brain.

Restlessly, he walked over to where Trask sat. The scientist looked up at him. His cheeks were pale, his eyes tired. 'David, I think you'd better put me under gas until this thing is over. I'm the Brain's pipeline to you. I heard all that – if it's hearing that's involved.'

Marin hesitated. It was a matter of intense interest to him what it was. But it didn't seem the right moment for a discussion about it. Nevertheless, he said finally, 'Would you say the method involves sound?'

'Yes. A circuit right in the hearing center, with a small speaker next to an ear bone.'

Marin nodded. 'That would certainly dispose of the need to consider mental telepathy – except for one thing. We've established that the circuit is in *your* brain. How do you account for *my* hearing it also?'

There was a strained look on Trask's face. 'David, someday listen to my theory about life and the duplication effect. But right now give me a shot from your gas gun. We're dealing with a creature as remorseless as man himself, and I'll be in the middle when it discovers that you're not going to play its game. For heaven's sake, man, be quick!'

Marin shot him with a twelve-hour gas charge. The scientist sank limply into his chair, and Marin walked slowly over to where the Great Judge sagged against the arm of his chair. He seemed to be sleeping peacefully. Marin looked up finally and said with a sigh, 'Gentlemen, we're going to have to keep him under until this battle is over.'

He added uneasily, 'I'm sure we can expect strong repercussions any minute.'

It was a few minutes before three o'clock when the Brain evidently realized that it was not going to have victory by agreement.

At that time sea patrol planes reported that five submarines had surfaced in the Gulf of Mexico, and each launched, one after the other, eighteen guided missiles. These subsequently attained a speed of thirty-four hundred miles per hour, and all headed at this enormous velocity for the Judge's City.

The patrol ships immediately attacked the submarines. They were met by the strongest antiaircraft fire, and more than half of the attackers were shot down. Air to sea missiles sent by the planes were somehow diverted and were exploded harmlessly far from the undersea craft. The remaining planes withdrew and contacted their headquarters for instructions. The submarines continued cruising on the surface for several minutes; then, as of one accord, they dived. They were not seen again.

Meanwhile, the missiles speeding toward the capital bypassed human perception by their sheer velocity. Automatic radar took over. Long, sliverlike defense missiles shot up from the ring of fortresses that surrounded the great city were electronically aimed, and set free to seek their targets. High in the stratosphere, ninety explosions occurred as, one after the other, the defensive missiles struck target.

The Brain, fighting for its existence, activated the warheads of the shattered missiles sent by the submarines. Seventy-two of them exploded. Seventy-two small, city-buster-size atom bombs exploded like a row of giant fire-crackers.

The shock wave was felt for a hundred miles, and the sound of it came vaguely into the Group Masters' building, where Marin and the council members remained in continuous session. They at this time had sounded the Deep Shelter alarm, and had already received a report of two other events.

'Dust!' A military plane radioed the message from a vantage point twenty miles outside the city limits. 'A dust cloud about thirty miles front. And it's rolling toward the city at about ten miles per hour.'

Just where it had started from was not immediately clear. Apparently it had been emitted from a long underground pipe line, from a secret storage supply.

The method of the defense forces was similar to that used to fight fire from the air. Planes swept back and forth over the dust cloud, spraying it with chemicals. Slowly, the 'dust' lost its unity and began to break up into small segments. These rolled unevenly, and not all one way. Finally, they were dissolved. Where they had passed, grass was brown-dead, all insects and other creatures were dead, all life had ceased to exist.

'To think,' said Elstan wonderingly, 'that it had all these devices hidden away for decades.'

Marin said grimly, 'Wait! There's more.'

The third great attack already had been building up.

It began to rain. Colored rain. Pink, blue, yellow, green. Marin watched it on the TV screen, and he was pale and shaken. Not for seventy-five years, not since the second atomic war, had such a rain fallen on a city of Earth. All through the third atomic war, hideous as it was, the belligerents agreed not to use the infinitely malignant droplets. Virus, germs, disease, plague – deadly, infectious. . . .

The technicians to whom Marin had given that section of Inskip's books dealing with the 'rain' had simply not had the tens of thousands of tons of anti-virus spray material that were necessary. And so, their makeshift defense was the automatic fire defense methods of turning on countless streams of water.

The water poured down from every building, and *onto* every building. Everywhere, the colored stuff was washed into the drains and down to the waste disposal plants. There, tons of pure virus were held up in the sludge. A gigantic task remained: to dispose of the incredible living death.

There were times, three quarters of a century before, when it had rained in color for hours on some of the world's greatest cities, so enormous was the quantity of virus available to the attackers, so determined were they to overwhelm the resources of the defenders.

This rain ended after eleven minutes.

Marin said, with relief, 'Evidently it can't really mount a big attack.'

Behind him, someone uttered a hissing sound of amazement. It was such a sound that it was instantly the most important and meaningful of voice expressions, demanding complete attention.

Marin spun on his heel. And then he said, in a staggered tone, '*Your excellency!*'

The Great Judge was sitting up. It was hours before the effect of the hypnotic gas charge, which he had had injected into him by the ultra-speed gas syringe weapon, was due to wear off. But he sat up, looked dazedly around, and said, 'I be defeated. It be my duty to give up. For human good, do not destruction I. I herewith cancel all instructions given I and clear all circuits for further instructions. Be sensible now, you councilors. I be wide open for future employment.'

Having delivered the message, the dictator sank back into his chair. He lay there, limp but breathing heavily.

There was a long pause.

'David!' it was Podrage, his voice strained. 'When the Great Judge later hears his own voice on the recording of this meeting, he'll know that he himself definitely was under the control of the Brain and that what you did here today was necessary. Since this is now an obvious truth, you may count on me, David. I'll stand behind you in what you did, and will not participate in or sanction any punishment for what happened today.'

There was a yell of approval and then a cheer from the others. They crowded around him, reaching for his hand, clapping his shoulder.

The excitement died down, and Marin walked over to his personal phone. With one hand on it, he said, 'Unless there is disagreement, I believe we are now in possession of a bona fide offer from the Brain, and I shall accordingly order Gregson to cease his attack and to wait for the Brain to open itself up.'

There was no disagreement.

When he had given the orders, Marin hung up and shook his head at Podrage. But he did not speak the thought in his mind. It seemed to him that the other Group Masters did not clearly realize what the Great Judge would have to do within himself to accept that he had been controlled by the Brain. The murder of so many many innocent persons, merely because they might know something about the Brain – even an absolute dictator might find that tremendously disturbing. He might even be inclined to blame someone rather than take the blame upon himself.

Marin said in a drab voice. 'I have the feeling that we have concluded all operations in the military theater. When his excellency comes to consciousness, will you tell him that I shall be at this address—' He wrote down Delindy's residence address, put it into an envelope, sealed it, and silently handed it to the other man.

They shook hands again.

CHAPTER FORTY-THREE

'He's still angry,' said Podrage on the phone. 'He refuses to see you.'

Marin hung up presently and walked out to where Delindy sat reading. He lay down on the grass at her feet and gazed thoughtfully at the hazy blue horizon. Nearly three weeks had gone by, and the fact was that he was lucky to be alive.

The young woman put down her book. 'Well?' she said.

Marin smiled at her gently. 'I think we can begin to assume that he's not going to murder me, my dear, sweet Andelindamina.'

He spoke the Jorgian version of her name tenderly. It was something they had resolved the very first day he arrived – her identity as the sister of the Queen of Jorgia. Confronted, she had admitted it without hesitation.

'I never did think he would do *that*,' she said, 'although' – there was a faraway look in her eyes – 'men have been known to destroy that which they love.'

'Particularly angry men,' said Marin. He shook his head. 'My dear Delindy, a real rage person has to have motivation to make him change his mind. I've seen these people; they hold grudges for entire lifetimes. Anyone who attempts to communicate with them is blocked. A bullet, or a blow with a sledge hammer – that can do it. Any real impact, emotional or otherwise, if delivered with enough force, can do it. Nothing else.'

'You're quite mistaken!' she said firmly. 'The Great Judge can be persuaded. I'll phone him. I'll talk to him.'

Marin felt the color creeping into his cheeks. 'I forbid it,' he said.

She bent down and kissed him lightly on the forehead. 'Dear David,' she said softly, 'I'm here with you because I want to be, not because you command it.'

She stood up decisively and headed into the house. 'I'll phone him.' She flung the words over her shoulder.

Marin remained where he was. His whole body was warm with jealousy.

The Great Judge said, 'David, I'm not exactly planning to retire. But I am now in a position where I have to think of a successor. I, also, will eventually grow old.'

Marin said, 'Sir, you have many great years ahead of you.'

He spoke a little stiffly. It was the morning after Delindy's call. They sat in the Judge's Court.

The dictator said, 'There are, of course, many possibilities. We may still rediscover the longevity drugs, despite their total destruction by my former comrades. But the fact is, we can discuss your role in the government at some other time. The principal reason I asked you to come over here today was because I have finally decided that Trask's group philosophy may have the answer for a problem that has been troubling me ever since I discovered seven months ago that you and Delindy were living together. At that time, I simply ordered her away from you.'

'Sir!' said Marin.

The color drained from his cheeks. He sat, shocked. It was the last subject he had expected to be brought up.

'You see, David,' said the leader quietly, 'there have been many, many secrets in my life — not the least was my early interest in having as many children as possible. I had scores before it dawned on me that I was extremely vulnerable to attack by my enemies through my children. So I hid my identity from them.

'I hid it from you. I hid it from your half sister, Delindy.'

Marin said huskily, 'I am your son? Delindy is your daughter?'

He added, in a vague voice, 'This is what you told Delindy . . . when she left me?'

'Yes. It was an error on my part not to have noticed who you were associating with.'

Marin parted his lips to speak again. But the feeling of shock was so great that no words came.

'I suppose,' continued the Great Judge, 'it was inevitable that, in our mating games, brother should sooner or later win an unsuspected half sister. This is becoming less and less possible, but the early recording system was not too clear. Briefly, when I asked for Darrell — as he called himself here — to be appointed ambassador from Jorgia, it was because I hoped to have his daughter, Delindy – my daughter, really – near me.'

Marin's body lost its numb feeling. His own background in this he knew much better than did the Great Judge. His mother and father had been captured early in the war. His mother had frankly confessed to him – after he grew up – that she had become the mistress of the Great Judge. She had told him that the dictator believed that Marin was his son, and she had added that he could expect many considerations from the Great Judge for this reason. 'But you are not his son,' she had said. 'Your father and I lived together much of the time when we were imprisoned, and it cost me quite a bit of trouble to so arrange it that his excellency later believed that you were his child. If he ever tells you, be surprised.'

Aloud, slowly, Marin said, 'The ambassador's daughter was really yours, sir? Your interest in Delindy was that of a father for a daughter?'

The dictator smiled. 'A wonderful girl. I feel proud to have such a daughter.'

Marin said carefully, 'How did the Jorgian ambassador ever agree – at the time – to such an arrangement between you and his wife?'

The strong face twisted into a smile. 'Come now, David, you know very well that it was wartime. He was with the forces. I found his wife at a moment when she was very much more worldly than she felt later. But it was my child, although she pretended to her husband that the baby was born prematurely.'

Marin did not doubt the identity of the parents. But that was not the confusion in this situation. Man of many secrets the Great Judge might be. But he didn't know that the sister of the Jorgian Queen had, for reasons of state, been substituted for the daughter of the ambassador.

Aloud, Marin said, 'You were saying that you feel there is a solution to these problems of consanguinity.'

The great man nodded. 'I've decided that we'll just have to take these chances.'

Marin hid his rising excitement. 'Your excellency,' he said wryly, 'am I to understand that you have decided to tolerate the marriage which I should like to undertake with Delindy Darrell, under the new laws which permit marriages of men with women who have had two children in the mating games?'

The Great Judge stood up and held out his hand. 'It's all a matter of attitude, David. I'm sure you two can be very happy.'

They shook hands.

'I'm sure of it also, sir,' said Marin.

He walked along the pathway, and he was thinking, It is only a matter of attitude. I am not his son, and Delindy is not his daughter. But because he *thinks* we are, it's just as if we truly were, so far as his feelings are concerned.

He sensed a great secret of human nature. Somewhere there was a thought, a feeling, that, if men would accept it, they would find the answer to their longings. They had sought it in such words as *comrade, brother, friend*, but these had always been briefly held ideas, quickly lost in the shadowland of history. Perhaps the binding glue of such feelings could be fortified by the new group relationships.

The strong, serious feeling faded. He found himself smiling, even a little gleeful. He recognized the exuberance for what it was, a sly sense of having won against many odds.

Nothing like putting something over on the old man! thought David Marin cheerfully.

THE END

Panther Science Fiction — A Selection from the World's Best S.F. List